the last leopard

'this third magical adventure about Martine and
Ben mixes high daring with a tale of true friendship.
The book is a real page turner.' *Carousel*

'St John's refined prose and assertive young
protagonists convey a profound regard for the
beauty and magic of the vast African backdrop
. . . a hugely enjoyable and gripping summer read'
The Bookseller

'another magical African thriller' *Times*

'A thrilling and enchanting story' *Lovereading*

Also by Lauren St John

The White Giraffe
Dolphin Song
The Elephant's Tale

Laura Marlin Mysteries

Dead Man's Cove
Kidnap in the Caribbean
Kentucky Thriller
Rendezvous in Russia

The One Dollar Horse trilogy

The One Dollar Horse
Race the Wind
Fire Storm

the last leopard

LAUREN St JOHN

Illustrated by David Dean

For Eve,
Thanks for introducing me at the Barnes Festival!

Orion
Children's Books

ORION CHILDREN'S BOOKS

First published in Great Britain in 2008 by Orion Children's Books
Paperback edition first published in 2009 by Orion Children's Books
This edition published in 2016 by Hodder and Stoughton

13 15 17 19 20 18 16 14 12

Text copyright © Lauren St John, 2008
Illustrations copyright © David Dean, 2008

The moral rights of the author and illustrator have been asserted.

A CIP catalogue record for this book
is available from the British Library.

ISBN 978 1 84255 667 2

Printed and bound in Great Britain
by Clays Ltd, St Ives plc

The paper and board used in this book are
made from wood from responsible sources.

MIX
Paper from
responsible sources
FSC® C104740

Orion Children's Books
An imprint of
Hachette Children's Group
Part of Hodder and Stoughton
Carmelite House
50 Victoria Embankment
London EC4Y 0DZ

An Hachette UK Company
www.hachette.co.uk

www.hachettechildrens.co.uk

For my godson, Matis Matarise Sandile Sithole,
in the hope that he grows up to love Zimbabwe
and its wildlife as much as I do . . .

And in memory of Felix and Michina,
my London leopards
1990 – 2007

Dawn was casting spun-gold threads across a rosy sky over Sawubona Game Reserve as Martine Allen took a last look around to ensure there weren't any witnesses, leaned forward like a jockey on the track, wound her fingers through a tangle of silver mane, and cried, 'Go, Jemmy, go!'

The white giraffe sprang forward so suddenly that she was almost unseated, but she recovered and, wrapping her arms around his neck, quickly adjusted to the familiar rhythm of Jemmy's rocking-horse stride. They swept past the dam and a herd of bubble-blowing hippos, past a flock of startled egrets lifting from the trees like white glitter, and out onto the open savannah plain. An early morning African chorus of doves, crickets and go-away birds provided a soundtrack.

For a long time Martine had only ever ridden Jemmy at night and in secret, but when her grandmother had found out about their nocturnal adventures she'd promptly banned them, on the grounds that the game reserve's deadliest animals were all in search of dinner after dark and there was nothing they'd like more than to feast on a giraffe-riding eleven-year-old. For a while Martine had defied her, but after several close calls and one terrible row with her grandmother, she had come to accept that Gwyn Thomas was right. When lions were on the hunt, the game reserve was best avoided.

Another of Gwyn Thomas's rules was that Martine ride sedately at all times. 'No faster than a trot and, in fact, I'd rather you stuck to a walk,' she'd counselled sternly.

Martine had paid almost no attention. The way she saw it, Jemmy was a wild animal and it was only fair that he should have the freedom to do what came naturally, and if that meant tearing across the savannah at a giraffe's top speed of thirty-five kmph, well, there wasn't a lot she could do about it. It wasn't as if she had reins to stop him. Besides, what was the point of riding a giraffe if the most he was permitted to do was plod along like some arthritic pony from the local stables?

Jemmy clearly agreed. They flew across the grassy plain with the spring breeze singing in Martine's ears. 'Faster, Jemmy!' she yelled. 'Run for your life.' And she laughed out loud at the heart-pounding thrill of it, of racing a wild giraffe.

A streak of grey cut across her vision, accompanied by a furious, nasal squeal: '*Mmwheeeh!*'

Jemmy swerved. In the instant before her body parted company with the white giraffe's, Martine caught a glimpse of a warthog charging from its burrow, yellow tusks thrust forward. Had her arms not been wrapped so tightly around the giraffe's neck, she would have crashed ten feet to the ground. As it was, she just sort of swung under his chest like a human necklace. There she dangled while Jemmy pranced skittishly and the warthog, intent on defending her young, let out enraged squeals from below. Five baby warthogs milled around in bewilderment, spindly tails pointing heavenwards.

The pain in Martine's arms was nearly unbearable, but she dared not let go. She adored warthogs – warts, rough skin, pig ears and all – but their Hollywood movie star eyelashes didn't fool her. In a blink of those lashes, their tusks could reduce her limbs to bloody ribbons.

'Jemmy,' she said through gritted teeth, 'walk on. Good boy.'

Confused, the white giraffe started to lower his neck as he backed away from the warthog.

'No, Jemmy!' shrieked Martine as the warthog nipped at the toe of one of her boots. 'Walk! Walk on!'

Jemmy snatched his head up to evade the warthog's sharp tusks, and Martine was able to use the momentum to hook her legs around his neck. From there, she was able to haul herself onto his back and urge him into a sprint. Soon the warthog family was a grey blur in the distance, although the mother's grunts of triumph took longer to fade.

Martine rode the rest of the way home at a gentle walk, a rueful smile on her lips. That would teach her to show off – even if it was only to an audience of hippos. At the game reserve gate, Jemmy dipped his head and Martine slid down his silvery neck as though she was shooting down a waterslide. That, too, wasn't the safest way of dismounting, but it was fun. She gave the white giraffe a parting hug, and strolled through the mango trees to the thatched house.

In the kitchen, brown sugar-dusted tomatoes were turning to caramel in the frying pan. Martine's nose wrinkled appreciatively. She was starving. Six days a week her grandmother served up boiled eggs and toast, with the occasional bowl of cornflakes as light relief, but on Sundays and special days like this she made up for it by cooking delicious brunches or roasts or allowing Martine to go for a campfire breakfast on the escarpment with Tendai, the Zulu game warden.

Martine took off her boots on the back *stoep* and stepped inside barefoot. "Morning, grandmother,' she said.

'Hello, Martine,' Gwyn Thomas said, closing the oven and standing upright. She wore a red-striped apron over a denim shirt. 'Wash your hands and come take a seat. Did you have a nice ride? Did Jemmy behave himself today?'

'Jemmy was an angel,' Martine responded loyally,

thinking: When does he ever *not* behave himself? It wasn't his fault if the warthog had woken up on the wrong side of her burrow.

There was a polite knock at the door.

'Ah, Ben,' said Gwyn Thomas with a smile, 'good timing. Breakfast is almost ready. Come and join us.'

'Thank you, ma'am,' said a clear young voice.

Martine turned to see a half-Zulu, half-Indian boy entering the kitchen a little shyly. He wore an army-green vest, heavy brown boots and ragged jeans – the only pair he owned since turning his others into shorts during an island adventure a little over a month earlier. He had glossy black hair and skin the colour of burnt honey and, though very slim – some might even say thin – he was sinewy and strong.

He rinsed his hands at the sink and sat down at the table. 'Have a bit of trouble with a warthog this morning, Martine?' he teased. 'You and Jemmy left skid marks all over the bush. The ground was so torn up it looked like the starting grid of the East Africa Safari car rally.'

'What happened?' demanded Gwyn Thomas. 'Were you going too fast, Martine? You know very well that you're expressly forbidden to gallop Jemmy. I won't have you breaking your neck on my watch. Ben, did the tracks show that she was going very fast?'

Martine glanced quickly at Ben. She knew that he knew she'd be in big trouble if she was caught racing the white giraffe, but she was also aware that he never lied about anything. Nor would she expect him to. She braced herself for a scolding and a temporary ban on riding Jemmy. Just her luck. And on the first day of the school holidays, too.

'I think . . . ' Ben shifted uncomfortably in his chair.

Her grandmother put her hands on her hips. 'You think what? Out with it, Ben.'

' . . . I think the toast is burning,' Ben said brightly.

Gwyn Thomas jumped up and seized the smoking grill pan, blowing on it to put out the flames licking at the four bits of charcoal that had once been bread. Just then the oven timer started beeping to indicate that the mushrooms were done and Martine noticed the tomatoes were starting to smoke. By the time they'd managed to rescue their charred breakfast, make more toast and hastily scramble a few eggs to go with it, her grandmother appeared to have forgotten about Martine's dangerous riding.

Ben distracted her further by relaying a warthog story Tendai had told him that morning, about an apprentice hunter he'd met during his game ranger studies. One afternoon the young hunter decided to entertain the other apprentices and demonstrate his bravery by tormenting a warthog in a game enclosure just for the fun of seeing her riled. He planned to hop over the fence if she came after him.

'Only problem was, the fence was electric!' reported Ben with a grin. 'The hunter was hanging on for twenty minutes, sort of sizzling, before she got bored and went away.'

Martine, whose arms still ached from her own encounter with an exasperated warthog, laughed, but not quite as hard as her grandmother.

'What do the two of you have planned for the holidays?' asked Gwyn Thomas, pouring them each a glass of paw paw juice. 'Apart, Martine, from riding the white giraffe very, very slowly.' She gave her granddaughter a meaningful glance, indicating that she hadn't forgotten what Ben had said but was prepared to let it go just this once.

Martine smiled gratefully. 'Don't worry,' she said, 'I'll be riding so slowly that even tortoises will overtake us.'

When she wasn't doing that she was hoping to brush up on her bushcraft skills and paint watercolours of the animals in Sawubona's sanctuary, a hospital and holding area for injured wildlife and new arrivals to the game reserve.

Ben, meanwhile, had his parents' permission to spend almost the whole holidays at Sawubona, studying under Tendai as an apprentice tracker.

When Martine first met Ben, he'd been almost completely silent, never speaking a word to anyone but her and his parents. Most kids at school had believed he was dumb. Some still did. But at Sawubona he seemed to really enjoy chatting to Tendai, Gwyn Thomas or anyone else who happened to be around.

As she listened to him describe his morning in the reserve, Martine absent-mindedly speared the last few potatoes on her plate and took in the scene in the kitchen. Eight months ago, her mum and dad had been killed in a fire in England on New Year's Eve and she'd been shipped like a parcel off to Africa to live with a strict grandmother she hadn't even known existed. For the first month or two Martine had been convinced she would never be happy again. Yet here she was sitting contentedly at the breakfast table with that same grandmother who, after a rocky start, had become one of her very favourite people, and with Ben, her best friend in the world apart from Jemmy.

Through the open doorway Martine could see zebras splashing around the distant waterhole. She would never stop missing her parents, but it definitely helped that her new home was one of the most lovely game reserves in South Africa's Western Cape and that she could ride through it on her own white giraffe and get close enough to zebras and elephants to touch them. She preferred the weather in Africa too. It was early but already the sun was spilling orange across the kitchen tiles and Shelby, the ginger cat, was stretched out in its warmth.

The telephone trilled loudly, making them jump. Gwyn Thomas checked her watch and frowned. 'It's barely seven o'clock. I wonder who's calling us so early on a Saturday morning.'

She went into the living room to answer it. Evidently the line was a bad one because she had to speak very loudly.

'Sadie!' she cried, her voice carrying clearly. 'What a lovely surprise. How nice to hear from you. How are things at Black Eagle Lodge . . . ? Oh, no. Oh, surely not. I'm very sorry to hear that. Well, if there's anything I can do, don't hesitate to let me know. *Excuse me?* Oh. OHHH . . . !'

Ben and Martine looked at each other, and Ben raised an eyebrow. 'Sounds like trouble,' he murmured.

'Uh, uh, yes, I understand,' Gwyn Thomas was saying. 'No, no, it's not an imposition. Please don't think that for a minute. In fact, the timing couldn't be better. We're on our way. Try not to worry. We'll see you very soon. Take care of yourself in the meanwhile.'

There was the sound of the receiver being replaced, followed by a long silence. When she returned to the kitchen, Gwyn Thomas's face was sober. 'Martine, Ben,' she said, 'I'm afraid you're both going to have to put your plans on hold. Martine, we leave first thing in the morning. We'll be gone for a month. We're going to Zimbabwe.'

2

Martine stared at her grandmother uncomprehendingly. 'Zimbabwe? What? Why? No, I can't leave Jemmy. I just can't. It's the beginning of the holidays.'

'I realize it's a bit of a bolt from the blue and I'm incredibly sorry,' said Gwyn Thomas, putting her hand on Martine's shoulder. 'It hurts me to disappoint you both. I know how you've looked forward to this time. I wouldn't entertain the idea of tearing you away from Jemmy or Sawubona if I could see any way of avoiding it. It's just that Sadie, one of my oldest and dearest friends, has had an accident and she desperately needs our help.'

'Do you mind if I ask what happened?' asked Ben. He

was just as crushed as Martine but was doing a better job of hiding it.

'Not at all,' replied Gwyn Thomas, sitting down and pouring herself another cup of coffee. 'Sadie runs a hotel called Black Eagle Lodge in the Matobo Hills in Matopos, one of the most remote regions of Zimbabwe. Matopos is famous for its extraordinary rock formations – great boulders that balance on top of one another – and also for its history. Many people believe that the lost treasure of Lobengula, the last king of the Ndebele people, is buried there.

'Unfortunately, a week ago Sadie slipped and broke her leg very badly. She has a plaster cast from her ankle to her thigh and is hobbling around on crutches. Zimbabwe is going through a hard time and life is very difficult for people there, what with crop failures and political problems. Last month Sadie had to lay off most of her staff. This accident means she's struggling to cope. Black Eagle used to be a popular riding centre, but now Sadie has only one man to exercise the horses and nobody to do the cooking or cleaning if any guests do show up. I thought that since Martine is a good giraffe rider and I'm a reasonable cook, it might be nice if we eased her workload for a month.' She gave Martine an appealing glance.

Martine pretended not to see it. She sat silently in her chair, arms folded, tears burning the back of her eyes. It seemed as if everyone and everything was continually conspiring to take her away from Jemmy. If she wasn't getting stranded on desert islands or being banned from

11

riding him, then poachers were trying to steal him. And now this. She couldn't recall hearing her grandmother even mention Sadie before, but all of a sudden she was claiming that Sadie was one of her oldest and dearest friends. Why couldn't Sadie find someone nearby to help her out? Zimbabwe was hardly down the road. It was over a thousand miles away.

There was no doubt that the Matobo Hills sounded intriguing, what with exotic rock formations and the Ndebele king's missing treasure, and she'd always longed to ride a horse, but given a choice she'd rather stay at Sawubona with Jemmy.

Ben, who knew how much it meant to Martine to be with her precious white giraffe, said, 'Is there anything I could do? I mean, maybe I could take Martine's place and come to Zimbabwe and do some work around the retreat. I've never ridden a horse before and I'd have to ask my mum and dad, but I'm sure I could learn, or at least feed the horses and muck out their stables or something. Then Martine could stay here and be with Jemmy. Umm, that is, if you'd like me to . . . ' His voice trailed away.

'Ben, that's extremely generous of you, but Martine can't possibly stay here on her own,' Gwyn Thomas told him. 'Tendai's much too busy to take care of her. And I'm not sure that your mum and dad would want you coming with us to Zimbabwe for four weeks – not to such a remote area. But if they do agree, we'd love you to have you with us, wouldn't we, Martine?'

Martine was torn. She didn't want to leave Jemmy, but

nor did she want Ben going off on an adventure without her.

'Martine,' said her grandmother warningly. 'Remember your manners. We'd love Ben to come to Zimbabwe with us, wouldn't we?'

'Ben knows that without me having to say it,' muttered Martine.

Normally Gwyn Thomas would have told her off for being so rude, but under the circumstances she just sighed. 'Martine, the last thing I want to do is make you unhappy or take you away from Jemmy. But I'm really worried about Sadie. I had the feeling that—' She hesitated. 'Maybe it's my imagination.'

'What?' Ben pressed.

'It's probably nothing, but I had the feeling that there was something Sadie wasn't telling me. She's the proudest, most independent woman I know, yet she practically begged me to help her. That's not like her at all. It made me wonder if something else is going on behind the scenes.' She took Martine's hand. 'I just feel she needs us. Do you understand?'

What could Martine say? Her grandmother had done so much for her.

'I'm sorry,' she said, giving Gwyn Thomas a hug. 'It's a bit of a shock, that's all. Of course I understand. I'll miss Jemmy terribly but it'll be great to see another country, especially if we can help Sadie and ride a few horses at the same time.'

'Wonderful,' said her grandmother with evident relief. 'In that case we should start packing immediately. We'll make a holiday of it. It's a long drive so we'll break it up with a night or two at Rainbow Ridge and other attractions along the way. Come with me, Ben. Let's call your mum and dad.'

She gave Martine's hand a squeeze. 'It'll be fun, I promise.'

Martine kept a smile on her face until her grandmother and Ben had left the kitchen. Then she walked out of the house and along the sandy track leading to the animal sanctuary, sat down beside the run housing two orphaned caracal kittens, and burst into tears.

She really did understand why her grandmother wanted to go to Zimbabwe to help a friend in need; she was quite sure that if she had a friend who was hurt or in difficulty, she'd react the same way. She just didn't see why she should have to go to the Matobo Hills as well. It wouldn't be so bad if Ben was allowed to join them, but if she had to be without both of her best friends for four whole weeks it would feel like a life sentence. Surely there was someone she could stay with right here in Storm Crossing. Someone like . . .

Martine stopped feeling miserable immediately. Why hadn't she thought of it sooner? She could stay with Grace, Tendai's aunt. Grace was a *sangoma,* a medicine woman and traditional healer with Zulu and Caribbean origins. Since she'd arrived in Africa, Martine had had a special relationship with her because it was Grace who'd first told her that she had a secret gift which would shape her destiny. 'The gift can be a blessin' or a curse. Make your decisions wisely,' was her advice to Martine only hours after she'd got off the plane from England.

The gift was a mystery even to Martine. She knew it had something to do with healing, and with a Zulu legend which said that the child who could ride a white giraffe would have power over all the animals. However, Martine, who'd recently been stung by a bee, and whose arms were still sore from the incident with the warthog, was quite sceptical about that particular detail.

Twice her future had been eerily mapped out on the wall of a cave. The paintings were hidden deep inside the Secret Valley, the white giraffe's sanctuary. On each occasion they'd made sense only after something had happened to her.

'That's not fair,' Martine had complained to Grace. 'If the San Bushman knew so much about my destiny, they should have made their paintings a lot easier to read. That way, I could avoid any bad stuff happening to me. For instance, if I'd known what was going to happen on the ship in June, I would have refused to set foot on it.'

'Exactly,' Grace retorted. 'If you could see your future, you'd only choose the good stuff, the easy stuff. Then you would never learn and never experience the important things in this world because oftentimes they's tha hard things. If you'd never gone on that boat, where'd those dolphins be now?'

'Ohhh,' said Martine. 'Oh, I see what you mean.'

Martine loved being around Grace, who was wise, funny, and full of fascinating knowledge about African medicine. She liked Grace's eccentric house, which had chickens wandering in and out, and she especially liked her banana pancakes. The only thing about staying with Grace was that Gwyn Thomas would probably return from her travels to find her granddaughter three times heavier than when she left. Then again, she might see that as a positive because she and Grace were always trying to fatten Martine up.

The more Martine considered it, the more of a good idea staying with Grace seemed. Grace was Gwyn Thomas's closest friend in Storm Crossing and she saw no reason for her grandmother to disagree. All that remained was to convince Grace herself.

The plan had hardly finished forming in Martine's mind when a voice with a pronounced Caribbean twang declared, 'I was jus' drinkin' tea with my nephew when I hear this terrible weepin' and wailin'. I says to myself, there ain't no reason for a chile, livin' on Sawubona under God's sweet sun, to be cryin' like the world is gonna end at midday. Let me see what's goin' on. And now I find ya smilin' and wit' mischief in your eyes. What's up wit' you, chile?'

The *sangoma's* sudden appearance at the exact moment she was thinking of her had the effect on Martine's mood of sunshine bursting through storm clouds. 'Grace!' she exclaimed, jumping up to embrace her. 'I was just thinking about you.'

Grace sank down onto the bench beside her. Usually she wore traditional dress, but today she was in a vivid pink skirt and top with a purple headscarf and matching purple shoes, an outfit made all the more eye-catching because Grace was a woman who'd indulged in many of her own pancakes. She looked at Martine expectantly.

Martine explained about her grandmother's Zimbabwe trip, ending with a heartfelt, 'Grace, I wanted to ask you a favour. Is there any chance I might be able to stay with you for a month?'

Grace was silent for so long that butterflies started to flutter around Martine's stomach. Surely Grace wasn't going to reject her? Finally the *sangoma* said, 'You can stay wit' me any time, chile, but not *this* time.'

Martine was taken aback and a little hurt, but having come up with the perfect plan she was not about to give up on it. 'I know four weeks is a long time, but I'll be as good as gold,' she promised. 'You'll hardly notice I'm there. I don't even need a bed. I can sleep on your sofa or your grass mat.'

But Grace's next words stopped her in her tracks. 'And what about the message from the forefathers. Ya goin' ta ignore that?'

'What message?' Martine began, and then it came back to her. In June she had been walking along a beach with her grandmother, Ben and his mum and dad, when she'd seen a leopard drawn in the sand. The image was so crisp and detailed, with even the whiskers and spots meticulously drawn, that it could only have been there a matter of minutes. And yet apart from a couple of fishermen unloading their catch in the distance and her friends, who'd gone on ahead, the beach was empty. She'd called Ben to come and see it, but in the split second her back was turned a wave had washed the sand smooth.

Martine could still remember the chill that had come over her when she realized the drawing had vanished, almost as if it had been meant for her eyes only.

The same chill went through her now. 'How could you possibly know about the leopard? I was the only person who saw it.'

'You must go to Zimbabwe,' Grace continued as if Martine hadn't spoken. 'What will be is already written. It is your destiny.'

Martine tried to decide whether the knowledge that none of the morning's events had been random – not the phone call, Sadie's accident, Grace's sudden appearance, not even, in all probability, the incident with the warthog – that it was all connected in some way, was comforting or infinitely creepy.

A gust of wind blew and two feathers floated out of the owl's cage. They twisted in the breeze and came to rest beside the bench, one lying across the other in the shape of the letter X. Oddly enough, they were not spotted and tawny like the owl himself, but jet-black and gleaming. Almost, Martine thought later, like the feathers of an eagle.

At the sight of the feathers Grace became extremely agitated. She seized Martine's arm. 'That boy,' she said urgently. 'The quiet boy, the Buddhist.'

Martine was startled. 'Ben?'

'Yes, yes, that one. You know now he is part of your story. You are bound together. When you journey to Zimbabwe, arl the time you must stay together. Any time you be separated, danger will follow you.'

Martine was used to finding Grace's predictions and warnings difficult to fathom, but this request struck her as both unreasonable and unrealistic. 'It's impossible for us always to be in the same place,' she told Grace. 'Ben likes to spend lots of time on his own, and he's always going off tracking. And anyway, his parents might not even allow him to come to Zimbabwe.'

But Grace was adamant. 'You *must* stay together,' she insisted. 'You must.'

Martine leaned back against the bench and closed her eyes. When she opened them again, Grace was putting the feathers into the leather pouch she wore around her neck.

'What does all this mean, Grace? Will I ever be able to have a normal life? I mean, I'm glad I have my gift, even if I don't exactly know what it's for, and I want to be able to heal as many animals as I can, but it would be nice if I could have just one school holidays where I could relax and read books and ride Jemmy and do the things that other kids do.'

Grace put a warm arm around her shoulders. 'How many kids have you seen ridin' white giraffes? Hmm? We don't always get to choose the paths of our lives, chile, and the path that be chosen for you is not an easy one. Trust in your gift. Your gift will keep you safe.'

The caracals began to fight over their food then, and Martine had to open their run and separate them. It only took a minute but Grace was already a splash of pink in the dusty distance, swishing away down the track without so much as a goodbye. As Martine watched, she lifted her hand and waved without turning her head.

Martine sat down on the bench again and stared unseeingly at the sanctuary animals: the caracals with their fur-tipped ears, the owl, Shaka the little elephant, and his new companion, a zebra foal who'd been rejected by his mother and was being bottle-fed by Tendai. She was thinking about the leopard in the sand. It had seemed an extra large leopard. It had been crouched, as if it was on the verge of pouncing. She could still remember its claws and the way its lips curled back over its teeth in a snarl.

The caracals started pacing about their run again, alerting her to footsteps. She looked up, expecting to see Grace returning, but it was Ben. A huge grin lit up his face.

'I've spoken to my mum and dad,' he said. 'I'm coming with you. I'm coming to Zimbabwe.'

So softly that only the caracal kittens heard her, Martine replied, 'So am I.'

3

Martine put down the book that she'd been attempting to read for the past hundred kilometres and hauled herself wearily into a sitting position. She was cramped, tired and slightly carsick, and her eardrums throbbed with the endless noisy hum of the Landrover. They had already been on the road for a day and a half and they'd shortly be arriving at Rainbow Ridge, where they were staying the night. Martine couldn't wait. Travelling was fun when there were fields of wildflowers or quaint historic towns to admire, but when there was nothing on view except a long, tapering ribbon of black asphalt, it was the most boring experience on earth.

'Is it far now? How long until we get there?' she kept asking Gwyn Thomas on the first day, until her grandmother threatened to play really loud opera music from there until Matopos if she dared raise the subject again.

They'd spent the first night at an ostrich farm midway between Cape Town and Johannesburg. Most ostrich farms bred the birds for their pocked, leathery skin, popular for belts and handbags, and also for their meat, but this one was a sanctuary for mistreated ostriches or those rescued from the slaughterhouse.

At dusk, Martine and Ben had sat on the rails of a corral and watched them strut around their paddock in clouds of sunset-tinted dust, their wrinkly necks gliding up and down like periscopes. The farmer told Martine that the great birds could be quite bad-tempered at times, and wouldn't hesitate to use their prehistoric toes to kick anything or anybody they disliked. They had an air of being very pleased with themselves, as if they thought everyone else at the farm was beneath them. They didn't seem at all grateful to have been rescued.

Martine's ears popped, and she became aware that the Landrover was climbing sharply. The mountains which had been a mauve outline for so long were all around them. Forested slopes gave way to sheer cliffs and crags and, just beneath them, a knife-edge ridge. Curlicues of smoke rose from it.

As they drew nearer they saw that the smoke was

actually mist caused by spray, and that a perfect rainbow arched over it.

'Rainbow Ridge!' said Ben, hanging out of the window with excitement. 'You can't see it from here, but beyond it is one of the highest waterfalls in Southern Africa. That's where we're going this afternoon, Martine. That's what we're going to climb.'

In the front seat of the Landrover, Martine, who was a fan of neither heights nor strenuous activity – not unless it involved giraffes – gave an involuntary shudder.

The campsite they were staying in was situated in a secluded valley well off the beaten track, so they were taken aback to find a buzzing throng of people around the reception desk. A photographer was snapping away and autograph hunters were circling. Gradually the crowd cleared to reveal two bearded young men in climbing gear. They had the healthy suntanned skin of outdoorsmen. A whispered enquiry revealed that they were Red West and Jeff Grant, famous Canadian mountaineers, who were on a tour of South Africa.

After a lengthy delay, the climbers moved off and their fans dispersed. A flustered receptionist checked Gwyn Thomas and the two children in and gave them keys to the log cabin where they'd be spending the night. She seemed quite overwhelmed by her celebrity guests.

'They're such gentlemen,' she said dreamily, 'and so handsome.'

Gwyn Thomas had difficulty getting her attention again. When she did, the receptionist had bad news. The campsite guides were all booked and there were no more tours to Rainbow Ridge until the following day.

'But it's an easy walk and very well sign-posted,' she said. 'As long as they're sensible, they'll be fine on their own.'

'I might be old-fashioned, but I really wouldn't feel comfortable allowing them to do a three-hour hike through forests and mountains with which I'm not in the least familiar,' was Gwyn Thomas's tart response. 'Unfortunately I've been driving for hours and don't have the energy to accompany them. Martine and Ben, I'm so sorry. Once again, I'm going to have to disappoint you.'

Martine was about to protest, not for her own sake but for Ben's, when the receptionist became all starry-eyed again.

'Excuse me, ma'am.'

They turned to see the taller of the two mountaineers. He introduced himself as Red.

'Forgive me for butting in,' he said to Gwyn Thomas in a Canadian drawl, 'but I couldn't help overhearing your dilemma and I wonder if my climbing partner Jeff and I might be able to offer our services. If Vicky here would be kind enough to vouch for us, we'd be glad to accompany these young people to Rainbow Ridge. We're on our way to the summit of the mountain range above it, so it's on our way. We won't be able to walk back with them, but we'll be able to show them the route.'

Vicky blushed furiously and was not able to give a coherent response, but a journalist who'd interviewed the climbers earlier assured Gwyn Thomas that Red and Jeff were men of impeccable character. He and the campsite manager persuaded her that Martine and Ben would be in safe hands.

Soon Martine and Ben were hiking through a pine forest with two of the world's most accomplished mountaineers, listening open-mouthed as Red and Jeff told stories about their epic climbs of the highest summits on seven continents.

'Which was the hardest?' asked Ben.

'Denali in Alaska,' Red replied without hesitation. 'There is something about hanging off an ice cliff in an Arctic wind that is uniquely terrifying.'

The track to Rainbow Ridge was, as the receptionist had promised, a straightforward and well sign-posted one, but after an hour of trying to keep up with the long strides of the mountaineers, Martine's leg muscles were screaming. She was thankful when they passed a picnic spot and Jeff declared himself starving.

'And I could murder a cup of tea,' Red agreed. Martine suspected that they were only stopping out of consideration for her and Ben, but she was not about to complain.

While Jeff fired up his miniature gas stove, Red dug out a kettle, teabags and sandwiches. Martine sat on a log, glad of a chance to rest and take in the scenery. Ben waited politely but they were within sight of the ridge and Martine noticed that he couldn't take his eyes off it. His eagerness made her smile. Ben always came alive in nature.

'You can go on ahead if you like,' she told him. 'I'll catch you up.'

'Would that be all right?' Ben asked Red and Jeff.

'No problem,' said Red. 'We're almost there anyway. Watch yourself, now.'

Ben bounced to his feet. 'Great, I'll see you in a few minutes.' He jogged off up the steep track.

The climbers were impressed.

'He's very fit, your friend,' commented Red. He switched off the gas stove and poured the tea. Jeff munched on a sandwich and rummaged through his rucksack. He wanted to show Martine a photograph of his children.

Ben grew smaller and smaller. He reached the top of the ridge and stood outlined against the rainbow and the hazy grey sky, mist roiling up all around him. As Martine watched, he leaned over the smoking void as if he was trying to see into the very heart of it.

Ben was the least annoying boy Martine knew, but she suddenly felt very irritated with him. What was he thinking, doing something so risky? His mum and dad would have a fit if they saw him teetering so precariously on the brink of a waterfall. Her heart began to thud in her chest.

'Sugar?' queried Red.

'What?' Martine blurted out. In her anxiety, she'd

forgotten about both tea and climbers. 'Oh, excuse me. No sugar, thanks.'

She took the mug from him, sipped some tea, and looked back at the ridge. Ben was no longer there. She shaded her eyes and scanned the horizon in case the clouds of mist and spray had temporarily obscured him, but he was gone.

Martine flung down the tea and leapt to her feet.

'Ow!' cried Red, as the scalding liquid splashed him. 'What the heck do you think you're doing?'

'He's fallen,' Martine heard herself say in a grown-up voice which didn't belong to her. 'Grab a rope, he's fallen.'

And then she was off up the twisting, rocky trail, running faster than she'd ever run in her life, her breath coming in short, painful gasps. When she reached the top of the ridge, it was immediately obvious what had happened. A jagged section of the overhanging bank was missing, as if a gap-toothed dinosaur had taken a chunk out of it. As Martine approached, a fresh shower of shale crumbled into the void.

'Ben!' she called, hoping against hope that there was a perfectly rational explanation for his disappearance. Red and Jeff were moving swiftly up the slope with their climbing gear. She lay flat on her belly, so that if another section of the bank broke off some part of her might be left on solid ground, and crawled towards the edge. The thunder of the waterfall filled her ears and mist drenched her face.

Steeling herself, she peered over the side. The

cascading rush of water ended over a hundred feet below in a foaming, sucking whirlpool. A ring of spiky rocks surrounded it like a fence of spears. The chances of Ben surviving either were zero.

'Ben!' screamed Martine hysterically. 'BEN!'

'Martine!' Ben's voice was so faint that it was barely audible against the roar. It seemed to come out of the ground beneath her stomach. 'Down here!'

Martine wriggled forward. There was nothing to grip on to and the yawning cavern gave her a strong feeling of vertigo, as though it was pulling her over the edge.

'Here,' Ben called again, and that's when she saw him. He was about thirty feet below, clinging to the withered grey trunk of a bonsai-shaped tree that grew sideways out of the rock. He didn't appear to be injured, but he was soaking wet and very pale. Several of the tree's shallow roots had been ripped from the rock by the force of his fall and the trunk sagged ominously.

'Ben!' cried Martine. 'Ben, hold on. Help is on the way.'

This time Ben didn't reply or move his head, in case the mere act of talking severed the tree's fragile grip.

Martine was inching her way back to safe ground when the climbers ran up.

'Where is he?' Red asked briskly. His eyes widened when Martine pointed over the brink.

The men went smoothly into action. With the ease of professionals accustomed to dealing with life-threatening situations, Jeff constructed a pulley system, using two jutting rocks as anchors, while Red made a harness from the other end of the rope and lowered it down to Ben. As he worked, he talked to Ben in a soothing, almost jokey way, explaining clearly to him what he needed do.

'Ben, I want you to pretend you're a spy. You're surrounded by laser lights which will trigger an alarm if you cross them. The only way for you to escape and get the bad guy is if you put this invisible cloak over your head – only you have to do it very, very slowly, using incredibly tiny movements. Great. You're doing brilliantly. Now slip the rope under your arms. Pull it a little tighter ... '

Without warning, several more roots ripped free from the rock. Ben lurched forward, almost losing his balance. He lay doubled over on the wet, slimy wood, breathing hard.

Red's tone never altered. 'Oops, don't worry, we've got you. Now I want you to sit up very, very slowly – remember the laser lights, you don't want to set off the alarm. Okay, hold on to the main rope with both hands and keep as still as you can. Ready, Jeff? Good. Here we go.'

Just as Ben's feet lifted clear of the grey trunk, the entire tree detached itself with a cracking noise that sounded like bones breaking. Wood, stone and moss plummeted into the smoking gorge. All four of them watched the tree shatter and nobody said a word. The thought that Ben could have fallen with it and been crushed by the force of water, impaled on the spear-like rocks, or drowned in the whirlpool far below, was too hideous to contemplate.

Red whistled through his teeth as he and Jeff hauled Ben up over the edge and onto solid ground. 'That was a bit too close for comfort,' he said, 'but you'd make one helluva spy!'

Martine was in such a state that she hardly knew how to react to Ben's safe return. 'That could have been you,' she said, throwing her arms around him. 'You could have fallen down there.'

'But I didn't,' Ben told her, gently extricating himself. There was a tremor in his voice, but otherwise he seemed remarkably calm. Aside from a few scratches and bruises, he was unhurt. He offered his hand to the climbers. 'Thank you so much for your help. I don't know what we'd have done without you. I'm sorry for causing you so much trouble and for delaying your climb.'

'No trouble,' Red assured him. 'Good thing we were around.'

Jeff eyed Ben's soaking clothes. 'You need to get those off and get dry as soon as possible. We'll walk to the campsite with you – you know, to make sure you get back in one piece. The mountain's not going anywhere.'

'We're fine,' Ben and Martine responded in unison.

'Thanks for offering,' Martine added hastily, in case they seemed ungrateful. 'My grandmother's waiting for us in one of the log cabins down in the valley. Don't worry, we'll go straight there. She was planning to light a fire, and make Ben some Rooibos tea or soup and get him warm.'

But the climbers insisted on taking them to the gates

of the campsite before saying their goodbyes. 'It isn't that we believe you can't get there quite safely by yourselves,' Jeff said. 'It's just that Ben has had a terrifying experience, and the combination of shock and cold can be as dangerous as any fall.'

Forty minutes later they were once more back at the campsite. 'Thanks for the tea and for rescuing Ben,' Martine said as the climbers turned to go. 'Sorry I burned you, Red.'

He smiled down at her. 'No worries. All's well that ends well,' he said, and Martine marvelled at the way he and Jeff were able to take a near-catastrophe in their stride.

It was only when the climbers were out of sight and Martine and Ben were alone that they began to take in what had happened. What *could* have happened. Ben started shivering quite badly and Martine, who felt responsible because she'd sat drinking tea while Ben went to the ridge on his own, was wracked with guilt.

'It's because we were apart,' she said in anguish. 'I should have stayed with you. Grace warned me. She said that any time we were separated during this journey, danger would follow us.'

'I know Grace is very wise,' said Ben, removing his wet fleece and rubbing his arms to generate some body heat, 'but it was nobody's fault but mine. I stood on the edge of a waterfall. It was a dumb thing to do. If it hadn't been for you, I'd be in bits and pieces at the bottom of Rainbow Ridge right now.'

Martine tried to block the image from her head. 'It

was Red and Jeff who saved your life,' she reminded Ben as they started down the mountain. 'I was so scared I could hardly even speak.'

'No,' Ben said, 'it was you. They had the equipment and the expertise, but if you hadn't acted as quickly as you did I wouldn't have been around *to* save.'

Martine had a sudden flashback of Ben as she'd last seen him before his fall. 'Why *were* you so close to the edge? What were you trying to prove? You seemed to be leaning right over it.'

Ben gave an embarrassed laugh. 'This is going to sound crazy. I thought I saw something, that's all. A picture – a sort of drawing. It was on the rocks, practically hidden behind the curtain of water. I couldn't really see it clearly, but it looked like a spotted wild cat of some kind. A leopard or cheetah or jaguar or something. I went closer to take a better look and that's when the ground gave way beneath me. I guess it was just my imagination.'

Martine's mouth went dry. She tried to think of a suitable response but none came. 'We have to stay together,' was all she could manage. 'Promise me we'll stay together.'

Ben saw that she was serious. 'Okay, okay,' he said, putting a reassuring hand on her arm. 'I promise.'

4

The remainder of the journey to the Zimbabwean border was uneventful. It wasn't particularly scenic, consisting mainly of long stretches of dry bush and scrubland; the fast, scary highways of outer Johannesburg, and ugly mining towns – *dorps*, Gwyn Thomas called them. Martine and Ben dozed until they reached Messina, where they stopped for a lunch of Hawaiian burgers decorated with juicy rings of pineapple, and chips slathered with spicy tomato sauce, all washed down with chocolate milkshakes.

Back in Storm Crossing, Gwyn Thomas refused to allow Martine to eat fast food, and she was at great pains to make it clear that this was a special one-off holiday treat. Martine had to hide a smile when the meal arrived and her grandmother tucked into her burger and fries with relish while doing her best to pretend that she really wasn't enjoying it at all.

'It's pretty good, considering that it's fast food,' Martine remarked innocently to her grandmother.

'I've had worse,' Gwyn Thomas admitted grudgingly, eyeing a passing ice-cream sundae with what looked a lot like envy.

She'd said very little about the incident at Rainbow Ridge, largely because Martine and Ben had said almost nothing about it themselves. On the way down the mountain, they'd decided that to mention Ben had nearly been killed falling down a waterfall would jeopardize the whole trip, which even Martine was now looking forward to. They'd told the truth but not, as judges say in courts of law, the whole truth. Ben had been very open about how he'd unwisely stood too close to the edge of the bank and tumbled headfirst into the water. He'd just left the word 'fall' off the end of 'water'.

He and Martine had received a mild telling off for taking unnecessary risks, but Gwyn Thomas's main concern had been getting Ben dry and making sure he had hot tea, a hearty dinner, and an early night in the cosy log cabin. Apart from being stiff and sore, he was as good as new today, and the trio were in high spirits when they reached the Zimbabwe border in the early afternoon.

'Are you treasure hunters or leopard hunters?'

demanded the customs official when he heard that they were on their way to Matopos. He studied them suspiciously over the tops of their passports, which he held fanned out like a poker player with a handful of aces. 'Treasure hunters, I think. You want to come to Zimbabwe to get rich?'

'We're doing nothing of the kind,' snapped Gwyn Thomas, trying and failing to keep the annoyance out of her voice. 'We're on our way to take care of a sick friend.'

'Ah, you are Good Samaritans?' He gave a smile worthy of a toothpaste advert. 'In that case, you are most welcome to Zimbabwe.'

It was a three-hour journey to Matopos, which stretched to four when they visited six different filling stations in the hope of finding fuel in Bulawayo, the nearest city. They drove through wide, curiously old-fashioned streets, overhung by jacaranda and flamboyant trees. Everything seemed to be in an advanced state of disrepair. There were potholes in the roads big enough to swallow whole cows. A friendly attendant at one of the garages where they stopped, who was sitting on a wall eating a banana in the absence of any trade, told them that the electricity worked for only four hours a day and it was nothing for the water to go off for days at a stretch.

'How do you manage?' Gwyn Thomas wanted to know.

'We make a plan,' he told her, and laughed.

Martine knew almost nothing about Zimbabwe, except that it bordered South Africa, was shaped like a teapot on the map, and was home to one of the seven natural wonders of the world, the Victoria Falls. Martine hoped the waterfall was a long way from where they were going. She was not in a hurry to see another one.

She'd learned a couple of new things in the few hours since they'd crossed the border. The first was that it cost millions of Zimbabwe dollars to buy three drinks. Martine had watched in disbelief as her grandmother counted out the notes.

The other was that 'Bulawayo' was the Ndebele word for 'place of slaughter'. The petrol attendant told them that the city was named after Lobengula's first big battle when he came to the throne – a battle in which his warriors were victorious. Martine thought it a creepy name for a town.

Their failed petrol search meant that they had to leave Bulawayo with the gauge almost on empty. Gwyn Thomas tried to put a brave face on it. 'I'm sure we'll be fine,' she said. 'The reserve tank usually lasts for ages and we don't have far to go.'

It was early evening when they reached the gates of the Matopos National Park. A park official unfolded himself from a makeshift table as they pulled up. He and three uniformed guards had been playing a game of drafts using bottle tops and a piece of cardboard on which they'd drawn squares with a red pen. Their rifles lay on the ground beside them.

'Good evening,' he said formally. 'It is after six p.m. The park is closed to visitors.'

'But it can't be,' cried Gwyn Thomas. 'We've driven all the way from Cape Town. We need to get to a ranch on the other side.'

'Eeeh, I'm sorry for that,' said the official, sounding genuinely sympathetic. 'You must spend the night in a hotel in Bulawayo and come back tomorrow.'

'We can't possibly do that,' she told him. 'For one thing, we can't afford it and for another we're almost out of petrol.'

'You have no fuel?' He tutted disapprovingly. 'It is not a good idea to come to the Matobo Hills with no fuel. Then you must sleep in your car and wait for morning.'

'But my friend is expecting us,' said Gwyn Thomas despairingly. 'Sadie – Sadie Scott at Black Eagle Lodge.'

Behind her, Martine saw the guards exchange a look, although what the look meant she couldn't tell.

'Sadie Scott?' repeated the official. There was a split second's hesitation before he continued warmly, 'Why didn't you just say so? Allow me to direct you.'

He drew the route on a tourist map, waved them through the open barrier, and the Matobo Hills were finally in front of them.

From the outset, Martine had expected the national park to be a disappointment. She'd been looking forward to hearing more about the Ndebele king's lost treasure, but as far as the rocks were concerned she'd been convinced that everyone was making a fuss about nothing. After all, how interesting could piles of boulders be? She'd pictured one or two particularly impressive rocky hillocks of the type Southern Africans called *kopjes* and pronounced 'kopies', maybe with monuments on the top, or one or two balancing rocks. Instead, there were hundreds, if not thousands, of geological marvels.

There were great stacks of teetering boulders – many leaning at angles that defied gravity, or sitting on perches a bird would have had difficulty balancing on. There were individual rocks as wide and high as mountains, and others shaped like animals or castles or faces. Some were thickly encrusted with jade and silver lichen, or streaked with orange or lime stains, as though they'd rusted in the rain. Others were smooth, grey and bare, with mysterious spaces between them suggesting caves or tunnels or vast, rainwater-filled hollows as big as Olympic swimming pools. Threaded through the rocks or surrounding them, were green tufts of African bush.

It was an awe-inspiring sight, and there was not a soul to witness it but the three of them.

'You'd think there'd be lots of tourists here,' observed Ben.

'You would think that,' agreed Gwyn Thomas, 'but I suppose people are nervous of coming to a place where it's hard to find petrol. I have to tell you that I'm beginning to feel the same way.'

The sun was setting, turning the tops of the rocks copper. Martine had never seen such a wild, lonely place. It made Sawubona seem as tame as a suburban garden.

'Look!' Ben said. A kudu bull and two kudu cows were

watching them with wide, almond-shaped eyes. As the Landrover passed, they took fright and loped away through the bush.

The park ranger's map indicated that they should turn shortly after passing a great baobab tree. Gwyn Thomas steered the vehicle off the main road and bumped along a steadily deteriorating track. The needle on the petrol gauge crept further into the red. All three of them noticed it happen, but nobody said a thing. The towering rocks seemed to close in on them. The potholes and craters worsened until Martine was sure that every tooth would be shaken loose from her head. Her grandmother fought to control the bucking vehicle. Martine felt for her. She was plainly exhausted.

After about a mile the track levelled and became smooth and sandy. They passed a village of five mud huts. Ngoni cattle with wide horns and hides so prettily patterned they might have been decorated by an artist rested in the dust. They chewed cud sleepily as they watched the Landrover go by.

At the edge of the village a crudely written sign indicated that Black Eagle Lodge was one mile ahead, beyond a gate and cattle grid.

Gwyn Thomas exhaled. 'Thank goodness,' she said. 'We'll be fine now. Living in such a remote area, Sadie's bound to have spare fuel.'

Ben hopped out to open the wire gate and they set off again. The grass along the edges of the track was overgrown and the trees crowded close, rapping the roof of the Landrover with their branches. Seedpods cracked and popped beneath the wheels. The air was muggy and still.

Martine began to feel claustrophobic. She was glad when they finally rounded a bend and found themselves in a clearing at the foot of an imposing, elephant-shaped mountain cast from a single slab of granite. Stone cottages with sagging, rain-darkened thatch were dotted around the foot of it. Two black eagles wheeled overhead. There was no other sign of life.

Gazing upon the empty scene, Martine was struck by the silence. There was something spooky about it. It was a silence so intense she could almost touch it and taste it. It swirled around her like a cloak of fog. It wouldn't have surprised Martine to learn that there was nothing at all beyond the mountain; that the landscape stopped right here. It was, she thought with a shiver, as if they'd taken a wrong turn, and found the end of the world.

5

Gwyn Thomas was the first to speak. 'Well,' she said huffily. 'I must say it's not quite the welcome I was expecting. Especially after a two-thousand-mile drive.'

But almost immediately a worried frown came over her face and she added, 'Oh, my goodness, what if something's happened to Sadie? I'd never forgive myself for not getting here sooner.'

Ben said, 'I think I just saw a curtain move.'

He didn't tell them what he'd really seen, which was what appeared to be a frightened face at the window of a house partially concealed by the mountain's long shadow, just in case he was mistaken and alarmed

Martine and her grandmother unnecessarily. Before he could make up his mind what to do next, the door of the house opened and an attractive woman, who appeared years younger than the sixty Gwyn Thomas had told them she was, swung out on crutches. She had on a floral sundress that had seen many summers. It flared over the bright pink plaster cast encasing her left leg and foot. The sandal she was wearing on the other foot had apparently been crafted from a piece of recycled car tyre.

'You can wipe that sour expression off your face for starters,' was her opening remark to Gwyn Thomas. 'I know what you're thinking. *"I've driven all the way from the Western Cape and Sadie hasn't put the welcome mat out."* Well, I'm sorry. Service is not quite what it used to be at Black Eagle, and it's even worse when I'm out the back trying to do the laundry on one leg.'

There was a brief pause, during which Martine expected there to be an explosion of some kind from her grandmother. Instead Gwyn Thomas's nut-brown face creased into a huge smile. 'I see that apart from the cherry-pink plaster-cast nothing much has changed,' she retorted. 'Still as crusty as ever!'

Then she rushed forward and embraced the other woman, taking care to avoid Sadie's injured leg. 'It's wonderful to see you, my dear,' she said. 'It's been far too long. Sadie, I'd like you to meet my granddaughter, Martine, and her best friend, Ben.'

Sadie hugged them both. 'Hello, Martine, and her best friend Ben. I've been counting the hours until you all arrived. When the sun started to set today with still no sign of you, I began to feel quite desperate.'

There was so much emotion in her voice that Martine, recalling her grandmother's words about Sadie being the proudest, most independent woman she knew, wondered if Gwyn Thomas had been correct in her suspicions that there was something more going on at Black Eagle than a broken leg.

'We came as soon as we could,' Gwyn Thomas responded. 'But I felt it only fair that Martine and Ben get to see one or two sights along the way.'

'Of course, of course. And I don't mean to sound selfish. I've just been so looking forward to your visit. Anyway, you're here now and that's all that matters. I'm actually surprised that the national park guards let you through the main gate. I've had a few difficulties with them recently. Having said that, one of my ex-employees recently started working on the gate and if you're lucky enough to come into the park when it's his shift, he's always a sweetheart.'

Her eyes widened as Ben and Martine began unloading bags of rice, buttermilk rusks and cans of guavas, smoked tuna and chopped tomatoes, along with their suitcases, from the boot of the car. 'What's all this?'

Gwyn Thomas smiled. 'I wasn't sure if there were enough groceries in the whole of Matopos to feed these two for a month. They might look undernourished, but given half a chance they'll eat you right out of Black Eagle Lodge!'

'You didn't have to do that,' responded Sadie,

laughing, 'but the more the merrier.' However, Martine noticed that she didn't protest.

As if suddenly reminded of her duties as host, Sadie exclaimed, 'You poor things, you must be worn out. Let me show you to your cottage.'

They ate dinner by candlelight. 'More romantic,' Sadie said.

Martine wondered if the real reason was that the electricity wasn't working, but decided it didn't matter. It was more romantic or, at least, more magical, to do everything by candlelight.

Night had fallen on the retreat with typical African abruptness. At 6:45 p.m. the red sun slid behind Elephant Rock, the mountain that gave Black Eagle its spectacular backdrop, and by 7 p.m. an ink-black darkness of the type only found in places far from city lights had descended. Sadie had shown them to their cottage along paths lit by cat's eyes, which, she explained, were solar-powered, and not dependant on the erratic power supply. There were three bedrooms, a lounge and a bathroom, all very simple, with faded curtains and threadbare rugs, but comfortable enough. The occasional gecko or blue-tailed lizard skittered across walls of glittering stone.

Over butternut squash stew, Sadie talked to them about the Matopos, an area rich in African history, much of it documented in the cave paintings found among the balancing rocks. Martine's ears pricked up at the mention of cave paintings, and for an instant she caught herself wondering about the likelihood of finding further clues to her destiny in Zimbabwe. But that, she told herself, was ridiculous, not to say egotistical. The San artists had had better things to do than go around Africa predicting the future of some white child they'd never heard of.

'Tomorrow morning, you'll meet Ngwenya, my right-hand man,' Sadie said. 'He's the groundskeeper and horse wrangler here at Black Eagle. He's also the only remaining staff member. Ngwenya is from the Ndebele tribe and he's much more of an expert on Matopos than I am, so you should save all your questions for him.'

Gwyn Thomas pursed her lips. 'Ngwenya? That's similar to the Zulu word for leopard – "Ingwe". Is there any connection?'

'There is. *Ingwenya* means leopard in Ndebele. Ngwenya has an ordinary name like you and I, but it's respectful to address him by his clan name. As a member of that particular clan he has a sworn duty to protect and honour all leopards, but that's a hard thing to do in these difficult times. We used to have the highest concentration of leopards in the world right here in the Matopos, but not any more.'

'Leopards?' interrupted Martine. 'Here? In the Matobo Hills?'

'Yes, leopards,' Sadie responded. 'Why? Are you particularly interested in them?'

Martine started chewing then, as if her mouth was full and she couldn't speak, so Sadie continued, 'Leopards are nocturnal which, as I'm sure you know, means they mostly hunt at night. They're the shyest and most elusive of the big cats. There are rangers in the Matopos who have worked here for twenty years without seeing one. For that reason it's very hard to keep a count of them.'

'You said you "used to" have a lot of leopards here?' said Gwyn Thomas. 'What happened to them?'

'Poaching and uncontrolled hunting has wiped them out.' Sadie's tone was bitter. 'And elsewhere some have simply starved to death because the animals they eat have also been poached and killed. They are on the verge of extinction in Zimbabwe. Here in Matopos, we know of only one. Few people have ever seen him but those who have say he is the largest leopard ever recorded. He is so cunning and elusive that the locals are convinced that when every other big cat in the country has been hunted down he'll be the only survivor. They call him Khan. They believe the day is coming when he will be the last leopard.'

'Have you ever seen him?' Ben asked.

Sadie glanced at Ben oddly, as if noticing him for the first time. 'Once,' she said abruptly. 'I saw him once, but it was so long ago I can hardly remember it.'

They were finishing their meal when Gwyn Thomas gave a tut of annoyance. 'Sadie, I forgot to mention that we're clean out of fuel. We did try to find some in Bulawayo but had no luck all. We limped up your driveway on the smell of an oil rag. I assume you keep some petrol on the premises.'

'I'm afraid not,' Sadie said. 'It comes in once a month. My next fuel delivery is not until – ooh, let me see . . . ' She stood up with the aid of her crutches and hopped over to a calendar illustrated with local wildlife. 'August 12th, it looks like.'

'TWO weeks away!' Gwyn Thomas burst out, but she caught herself and added more politely, 'That's not for nearly a fortnight. What if there's an emergency? What if we want to take a drive around the Matobo Hills?'

'That's what the horses are for,' Sadie told her cheerfully, and Martine had the distinct impression she wasn't exactly sorry that they were stuck here at Black Eagle for weeks on end – probably wouldn't be sorry if they were stuck here forever.

'This is a disaster,' cried her grandmother.

'Gwyn, Gwyn, Gwyn,' Sadie scolded reproachfully, as if Gwyn Thomas was a misguided child. 'You're on holiday now. I'm sure you haven't had a proper break in years. I'm aware that I've asked you to help me run the retreat for a month and that there'll inevitably be a few mundane chores each day, but the present lack of visitors means there should be plenty of time to relax. At least it's peaceful here. Matopos is so isolated that it forces you to forget about the modern world for a while. We have no television or email, and the phones are hopelessly unreliable.

'As for emergencies, Zimbabweans have a saying: "Make a plan." It's our national motto. It means that no matter what life throws at you, you keep smiling and figure out a solution.'

47

'You might have a point, Sadie,' said her friend. 'I'm so used to my routine at Sawubona, where there are always visitors arriving or animals needing attention, that some enforced rest and relaxation might do me the power of good. It won't do Ben and Martine any harm either. They're still recovering from a disastrous school trip they took in June. We're definitely all in need of a holiday. If we have to wait a few weeks for the fuel to arrive, then so be it.'

Martine caught Ben's eye and saw he was just as stunned as she was. It was one thing being at the end of the world by choice. It was a totally different matter being stranded there.

Later, Martine was climbing into bed in her pyjamas when she remembered she'd left her survival kit hanging over the back of her dining room chair. She was so sleepy that she was tempted to leave it till morning, but Tendai had drummed into her the importance of having it with her even when she least expected to use it. 'Keep your survival kit with you for when you need it most, little one,' he always said. 'When you need it to survive.'

Ben and her grandmother had turned off their lights, so Martine tiptoed out of the cottage and along the path to Sadie's house, which also served as the retreat reception, lounge and dining area. Cat's eyes lit the way. The kitchen door was ajar. The survival kit was exactly where Martine had left it. Out of habit, she wrapped the pouch around her waist and secured the Velcro straps. She was hurrying from the building when she heard Sadie's voice raised in anger. Surprised, Martine crept back along the passage and put an ear to the lounge wall.

Sadie was on the phone. 'I don't want your blood money,' she was saying furiously. 'I want you to leave us alone. Nothing you can say will change my mind. *Ever.* Over my dead body will you take him.'

She slammed down the receiver, and there was the clack of wood as she gathered her crutches. Martine darted out into the night. A key turned in the lock and the kitchen windows went dark.

Despite her tiredness, Martine was awake for a long time, replaying in her mind what she'd heard. Who was threatening Sadie and why? 'Over my dead body will you take him,' she'd said. That was a very extreme statement. Who was the 'he' Sadie was protecting? Who did 'they' want to take? Even more disturbing was the comment about blood money. Was Sadie being blackmailed in some way?

She was just drifting off to sleep when the silence was split by what, even through the fuzziness of half-consciousness, she recognized as a leopard's roar. But it was no ordinary roar. It was an expression of rage and absolute defiance, both the protest of a savage, untamed creature and a declaration of war, and it touched the very core of Martine's being.

When she woke up in the morning, she had no idea whether or not she'd dreamt it.

· 6 ·

Tuk-tuk-tuk. Tat-tat-tat. Tuk-tuk-tuk. Tat-tat-tat.
'Come in!' Martine shouted for the fourth time,
her voice cross and thick with sleep. She couldn't
believe it was already daybreak and she was very
annoyed with whoever it was who kept knocking but
refusing to enter. It was only when she took the pillow
off her face and sat up that she realized the sound was
coming from the window rather than the door.

She pulled back the curtain. A black and white-
speckled hornbill with a big yellow beak was staring in
through the window. As Martine watched, its beady eyes
slid to her survival kit. She'd opened it to take out her

torch the previous night and it was still lying on the ledge.

'Don't get any ideas,' Martine told the bird, zipping up the pouch and tucking it under her pillow, out of view. She checked her watch and yawned. 'And next time wait until at least seven o'clock before you even think about waking me up.'

'That's Magnus,' Sadie informed her over a breakfast of butternut fritters and scrambled eggs prepared by Gwyn Thomas. 'He loves shiny things and he's an awful thief, so watch your possessions. The locals say that the person who finds Magnus's nest will be able to feed everyone in Matopos for a year there'll be so many rings, rubies and riches in it. But so far he has managed to outwit us all. I have to warn you he gets very attached to visitors. Don't be surprised if he starts following you around.'

Martine studied Sadie from under her fringe, but although her grandmother's friend had dark circles under her eyes and seemed a touch distracted, she made no mention of the telephone row the previous night. If she was being blackmailed or threatened, she certainly didn't show it.

'"Over my dead body will you take him." Are you sure that's what you heard?' Ben asked as they walked down to the stables after breakfast. Magnus the hornbill accompanied them, waddling ponderously alongside.

'I'm not a hundred per cent certain, because I was tired and listening through a wall,' admitted Martine, 'but I'm pretty sure. And anyway she definitely made the comment about blood money.'

They followed the path through a grove of gum trees. The smell of horses, Martine's favourite next to giraffe breath and baking bread, grew stronger. In front of her, Ben halted. The hornbill paused at the same time. On the far side of the stableyard, Sadie was in deep conversation with a man they assumed was Ngwenya. Their heads were close together and their expressions were serious.

'Maybe it was Ngwenya who Sadie was referring to on the phone,' Ben said in a low voice. 'It could be that somebody's trying to tempt him away to a better job and she's doing her best to hold on to him. She did say he was her right-hand man.'

Before Martine could answer, Sadie's companion spotted them. He murmured something to Sadie. She motioned them over with a crutch.

'Martine, Ben, let me introduce you to Ngwenya. Black Eagle would have gone out of business long ago if it weren't for him.'

Ngwenya shook their hands with calloused, sun-warmed palms. 'Gogo is being too kind,' he said. 'She would get along very well without me.'

'*Gogo* means grandmother in Ndebele,' Sadie explained, seeing their puzzled expressions. 'It's a term of endearment and respect used for all older women. And no,' she said fiercely to Ngwenya, 'I couldn't manage without you. I just couldn't.'

Ngwenya chuckled. 'Come and meet your new friends,' he said to Ben and Martine. 'You are good riders, yes?'

Ben shook his head. 'I've never ridden a horse in my life.'

'And I've only ever ridden a giraffe,' Martine said.

The horse wrangler smirked and waited for her to finish the joke. When she didn't, he glanced at Sadie as if to say, 'Is your friend's granddaughter in the habit of making up such ridiculous fantasies?'

Sadie laughed. 'I've never actually witnessed it, but I'm told it's true. On the game reserve where she lives in South Africa, Martine rides a giraffe called Jemmy.'

Ngwenya clapped a hand to his forehead. 'A giraffe!' he exclaimed dramatically. 'You ride a giraffe?' He examined Martine with a great deal of interest. 'With horses,' he said, 'I think you will be a natural.'

As it turned out, he was an excellent judge of potential. For most of her life Martine had been hopeless at every sport she'd ever tried apart from giraffe riding, but she swung into the saddle as if she'd been doing it since the day she was born. Everything came easily to her. Everything *was* natural. After months of learning to stay aboard a ten-foot-high wild giraffe – one who had a disconcerting habit of making unexpected detours to snatch at clumps of juicy acacia leaves, sometimes in mid-gallop – riding a schooled, responsive horse was a breeze.

Mounting and dismounting using stirrups was simplicity itself, and Martine bumped only twice before mastering the rising trot. But the thing that really impressed Sadie and Ngwenya was her affinity with Black Eagle's six horses. So tranquil did they become when she touched them that after ten minutes of watching her ride Jack, a big-boned black horse, Ngwenya declared that it would be her responsibility to exercise Sirocco and Tempest during her stay at the retreat.

Sirocco and Tempest were highly strung Arabs, with arched necks, dished faces and delicate, flaring nostrils, but once Martine had saddled Sirocco under Ngwenya's expert guidance and trotted her round the paddock, the chestnut mare became positively placid.

Ben, meanwhile, was having a terrible time. It's not that the horses disliked him; Ben was so gentle and treated animals with such kindness and respect that the opposite was true. It's just that Cassidy and Mambo, the pot-bellied white ponies Ngwenya had told him it would be his duty to exercise, sensed that he had no idea what he was doing and played up mercilessly.

Hardly had they rounded Elephant Rock than Cassidy shied at some imaginary object and threw Ben off into a bush. And every few strides she'd pause to snatch mouthfuls of grass, or make a dash for home. Eventually, Ngwenya attached a lead rope to her bridle and she was forced to accompany him and Jack. She did it meekly but reluctantly, with lots of yawning and snorting.

One part of Martine felt sorry for Ben, but then again he excelled at so many things – he was a straight A student, Caracal Junior's cross-country running champion, a gifted swimmer, and wonderful at wilderness activities like building shelters and fishing – that it was quite nice to find a chink in his armour. Still, she didn't like to see him struggle so she helped him as much as she could.

There was something about negotiating Matopos's extraordinary terrain on horseback that made it all the more spectacular. They felt connected to it. In daylight, the intense silence was not creepy but simply peaceful, and as Martine adjusted to the short, bouncy strides of Sirocco, so different from Jemmy's long lope, a calm feeling came over her. Sadie had told her that the Matopos was the spiritual home of the Ndebele tribe and she could understand why. The domes and spires of the boulders were like a living force all around them. When they reached a high point, distant *kopjes* unfolded in watery blue and violet layers against the horizon.

Not long after they set off, they came across two girls – one six-year-old and one aged eight, neatly dressed in dark green school uniforms. Martine and Ben couldn't hide their astonishment. There was not a building in sight. The girls were strolling through the thick bush with their exercise books under their arms, as if it was perfectly normal for Zimbabwean children to walk unaccompanied to non-existent classrooms through lonely areas teeming with wildlife and poisonous snakes.

Ngwenya spoke to them in Ndebele and they stared up at Martine and burst into fits of giggles, covering their faces shyly with their books. They went on their way with smiles and waves, pausing periodically to look back over their shoulders and giggle some more.

'I told them that your usual horse is a giraffe,' Ngwenya explained to Martine. He added that not only did the girls walk alone through the bush almost daily, they walked an incredible six kilometres to school and six back during term time.

'Why?' asked Martine, bewildered. Six kilometres was more or less the distance from Sawubona to Caracal Junior, and even that journey seemed to take forever in Gwyn Thomas's car. Martine didn't much like school, which gobbled up time she'd have much preferred to spend riding Jemmy, and she couldn't imagine wanting to go to class so badly she'd risk life and limb to walk twelve kilometres on her own.

'Because their parents are poor and have no car.'

'No, I mean, why do they go all that way by themselves?'

Ngwenya shrugged. 'They are hungry to learn. They want to grow up to be doctors or scientists. They have seen the life of their parents, who are unemployed or tend goats or cattle, and they want something better for themselves.'

Martine immediately felt guilty that she didn't have a better attitude towards school. She made up her mind to be more appreciative in the future and to try harder in lessons.

The bush they were riding through seemed jungle-thick and untouched, almost as if they and the schoolgirls were the first human beings ever to cross it. But according to Ngwenya there'd been human beings in the area for over 40,000 years. Many tribes had come and gone. The Banyubi hill people had been followed by a whole mix of Mashona and other tribesmen, most of whom fled or were conquered when Mzilikazi, the first Ndebele king, came to the Bulawayo and Matopos areas in 1839 with his wives and warriors.

'Mzilikazi called this area "Matobo" because the rocks reminded him of the heads of bald men,' Ngwenya said.

Martine smiled at him as she considered this. She liked Ngwenya, who had an open, pleasant face. There was nothing particularly striking about him. He was of medium height and build and was the sort of person you would pass without noticing on the street. But he had an infectious laugh, like an especially cheerful bird, and was a man she felt she could trust implicitly.

They were winding their way along a narrow path when Ben saw a splash of colour ahead. 'What's that?' he called to Ngwenya.

Ngwenya reacted as if he'd been poked with something sharp. 'Get down! Get down!' he hissed, leaping off Jack and pulling the horse into a thicket of trees. Martine and Ben barely had time to do the same with Sirocco and Cassidy before three men came striding along the path in the opposite direction. The one in front was wearing a trilby hat and a shirt with the sleeves rolled up. The others were in overalls, open to the waist. Their muscular bodies, shining with sweat, could have been carved from wood. One had a heavy sack of maize meal on his head; the others were loaded down with equipment. They were arguing about something and didn't notice the horse tracks.

'Looks like they're trying to find some kind of metal,' Ben said softly to Martine. 'The man in the hat is carrying a metal detector.'

'Are you sure?' Martine watched as the men followed the path around a dinosaur-shaped boulder and disappeared. 'What if they're poachers?'

'They are not poachers, I can promise you that,' Ngwenya said. He sounded almost angry. 'One is my uncle's son. He is my cousin.'

'Why are you avoiding your own cousin?' asked Ben.

'He is not a good man,' Ngwenya replied. 'He and his *shamwaris*, his friends, are *tstotsis* – troublemakers. They do not want to find a job; they want to find the treasure of Lobengula.'

'Does that mean it's true? The story of the king's lost treasure?'

Ngwenya grimaced. 'So you have heard about it. Yes, it is true.'

'Can you tell us something about its history?' Martine pleaded. 'How did the treasure go missing? What exactly is it? Is it precious jewels?'

Ngwenya sat down in the shade and leaned against a tree. He took a packet from his pocket and offered them some dried mango. 'Make yourselves comfortable,' he said. 'I will tell you what I know.'

7

According to Ngwenya, Mzilikazi and his followers had travelled 500 miles and taken ten long years to reach the hills they called Matobo from their original home in South Africa. It was a journey known as the 'Pathway of Blood', so many battles did they fight along the way. Mzilikazi had been the Zulu king Shaka's bravest and most brilliant lieutenant. When his popularity grew too much for Shaka, the Zulu king wanted to have him murdered. Mzilikazi fled, taking his wives and loyal warriors with him. His fighting skills and those of his men were so legendary that their enemies called them the AmaNdebele, 'People with Long Shields'. They became known as the Ndebele: 'The ones who followed' or even 'Children of the Stars'.

Mzilikazi reigned successfully for nearly two decades in the Matobo Hills and his reputation as one of the greatest African kings of all time spread throughout the continent. But when he died it was found that his eldest son, the heir to his throne, had mysteriously vanished. All efforts to locate him failed. After a debate lasting two years, a council of *indunas*, chiefs, appointed Lobengula, Mzilikazi's son by an inferior wife, as his successor in 1870.

Lobengula's nickname, *Ndlovu*, meant 'Great Elephant' and he grew to embody it, standing well over six feet tall and filling out until he resembled a bull elephant. He was almost as great a warrior as his father and successfully led a rebellion against the white settlers, but some suspected him of having several of his own brothers murdered and distrusted him greatly.

'But what about the treasure?' Martine said impatiently. She had a low boredom threshold with history. 'Where did the treasure come from?'

Ngwenya laughed. 'You want me to "cut to the chase", as the American tourists say?' He ate another piece of mango before continuing.

'The treasure came from raids on other tribes and from gifts from the Colonial hunters, miners, and explorers. The elders say he had three tins filled with diamonds, raw gold from the mines of the Mashona, and many bags of British and Kruger sovereigns. He also had much ivory. I have heard it told that some nights he would order his secretary, a white man from Cape Town called John Jacobs, to cover his body in gold sovereigns from head to foot.

'One day he came rushing from his house and gave orders for his treasure to be taken into the bush to a safe place. Lobengula, Jacobs and four *indunas* went with the treasure on the wagons, followed by the fourteen Matebele who would bury it. They hid it well and sealed the entrance with a stone wall. When they returned that night, Lobengula ordered all who had buried the treasure to be killed in case they had thoughts of stealing it. Many were slain but some escaped . . . '

A baboon's eerie cry, 'Qua-ha, qua-ha-ha!' suddenly split the silence. Ben and Martine, who were absorbed in the story, jumped at least an inch off the ground. Ngwenya rapped a stick loudly against the trunk of the tree and the rest of the troop loped away, the babies riding high on their mothers' backs. The male baboon took his time following, pausing to scratch a flea and eat a few imaginary berries for their amusement. 'I'll go when I'm good and ready,' he seemed to be saying.

'Did any of those who escaped ever say where the treasure is buried?' Ben asked Ngwenya.

'If they did, each person took the secret to the grave. After Lobengula's death, John Jacobs led many expeditions into Southern Rhodesia, as Zimbabwe used to be known, to try to recover it, but each time the expedition was cursed as the witchdoctors, traditional healers and fortune tellers – they are like your *sangomas*, I think – had foretold it would be. Men were struck down with illnesses none had ever seen before; charged by elephants or murdered by rivals; one even had his nose licked by a lion. The same fate befell others who tried to find Lobengula's surviving *indunas*. Jacobs was sentenced to hard labour for entering the country without the proper permit.

'Some people believe that the treasure is definitely in the Matobo Hills. Others say it is in the Batoka Gorges or as far away as Zambia. Over the years hundreds of people have come in search of it. We have seen Englishmen with maps drawn by their great-great-great-grandfathers; descendants of Lobengulu's *indunas*; Zimbabwean officials; Japanese tourists; Russian geology experts; Australian archaeologists. Nobody has found any trace of it.'

His gaze shifted to the path taken by his cousin. 'Many good men have been driven crazy by this quest.'

'Then what makes your cousin and his *shamwaris* so confident they can find it?' asked Martine, surveying the mountainous landscape. Hunting for a needle in a haystack would be nothing compared to searching for the treasure troves of Ndebele royals in this Land of a Thousand Hills.

Ngwenya's reply chilled her to the bone. 'They believe that the leopard they call Khan will lead them to it.'

'What do you mean?' Martine said.

The horse wrangler was clearly uncomfortable talking about it. He kept checking uneasily over his shoulder as if he thought his cousin was about to pop up from behind a rock and smite him to the ground for saying the words out loud. At last he said, 'Can you keep a secret?'

Martine nodded furiously, and Ben gave his word.

Ngwenya looked around once more before continuing in a low voice, 'They have spoken with our local witchdoctor, and he has told them that the last resting place of the king of leopards is the hiding place of the king's treasure.'

Martine swallowed. 'The *last* resting place. You mean . . . ?'

Ngwenya's mouth twisted. 'Exactly. I mean that before the treasure can be found the leopard has to be dead.'

8

For most of the next week, they rode twice a day, going out on Sirocco, Jack and Cassidy in the morning and Tempest, Mambo and a thoroughbred called Red Mist in the evening. Ben's riding improved and he slowly developed the right muscles, stopped being quite so saddlesore and was able to sit down again at meals.

They always went out with Ngwenya who, they found, had the dry humour that characterized many Zimbabweans. He would tease them about the local tree that was said to chase naughty children in the night, and was very funny on the subject of past guests at Black Eagle Lodge.

'If a bird watcher comes, that's when you know you are in for a bad day,' he said, his Ndebele accent turning *birds* into *beds*. 'These people, they only want to see small beds, big beds and medium beds. Even if you see a lion chasing something, they don't mind. Even if one elephant is killing another, they don't mind. They only want to see beds. You need a lot of patience because they will look in their book, "Oh, it's the Blue-Mantled Crested Flycatcher!"'

Ngwenya was as good a guide as Sadie had boasted. One afternoon he showed them grain bins used by the Bushmen, and biting ants so fierce they were known as the Enemy of Lions. 'Where you find these, you won't find any lions. Even snakes, you won't find them here.'

The shadows were lengthening by then, so they turned the horses in the direction of the retreat and threaded their way through the balancing rocks and bush-filled gullies. The air was filled with the exotic scents of plants and animals and the woodsmoke of unseen villagers in faraway huts preparing their evening meals.

Twice Martine thought she saw a streak of gold in amongst the foliage on the knobbly hills, and she found herself wondering if the leopard was watching them. She had been incredibly distressed by the story of Ngwenya's cousin and had found it hard to understand why the witchdoctor would tell men who obviously had ulterior motives that it was only when the leopard was dead that they'd find their treasure.

'Doesn't the witchdoctor have an obligation to protect

the leopard if he is a member of your clan?' she asked Ngwenya.

But the horse wrangler had explained that, although he and the witchdoctor were both from the Ndebele tribe, the witchdoctor was from a different clan.

'Even so, it seems wrong that he would tell them something that might tempt them to go out and kill the leopard,' Martine said.

'I agree,' was Ngwenya's response. 'But not all witchdoctors do things for the right reasons.'

Riding beside Ben now, Martine scanned the hills for any sign of the treasure seekers, the leopard or even a leopard spirit. She hadn't been able to think about the Matobo Hills in quite the same way since discovering that they were riddled with shrines created by the early Mashona tribesmen, who had worshipped Mwali, the High God. Each shrine had its own guardian and they were looked after to this day.

Ngwenya had many stories about ghostly goings on amid the rocks and hills, which he said were full of spirits. He claimed that Lobengula had regularly visited the Umlimo Cave on Mount Injelele, the Hill of Slippery Sides, to consult a spirit which could 'bark like a dog, crow like a cock or roar like a lion'.

'The pilgrims who visit the shrines often say they hear the voice of Mwali coming from the rocks,' Ngwenya said. 'You might even hear it yourself. But don't worry; the "Voices of the Rocks" also has a scientific explanation. The boulders expand in the sun and shrink at night when it is cool. When they get smaller, they moan or growl like thunder.'

Martine listened hard but could hear nothing but the faint whistle of the wind through the rocks and crags.

Ngwenya explained that each shrine had its own guardian or messenger who was in communication with Mwali or the cave spirit, and that one famous shrine messenger, a seven-year-old girl, had lived underwater at Dzilo shrine for four years 'just like crocodiles do'. The spirit had taught her good manners, how to be humble and kind-hearted, and how to teach others to live in harmony with nature.

Martine could think of quite a few pupils at Caracal Junior who would benefit from the teachings of such a spirit, but she found it hard to credit that an intelligent man like the horse wrangler could actually imagine that a young girl could spend four years underwater like a crocodile.

'But surely you don't believe that?' she pressed Ngwenya. 'Surely you don't believe in the supernatural?'

He looked at her in surprise. 'These things are not supernatural,' he said. 'These are our truths and the truths of our ancestors.'

On their sixth day in the Matopos, Ngwenya and Sadie decided that Martine and Ben were familiar enough with the landscape around the retreat to be trusted to go out alone. Gwyn Thomas was concerned but Sadie assured her that as long as they stayed on Black Eagle land and didn't venture into the national park, they were unlikely to run into anything more deadly than an antelope.

'Provided,' she cautioned them, 'that you don't go near the northern boundary fence. Rex Ratcliffe runs a hunting and safari operation on his ranch, the Lazy J, just the other side of it. They're a trigger-happy lot and I wouldn't want you getting shot by mistake.'

Martine could tell that her grandmother didn't appreciate her friend's humour. It wasn't until later that it struck her that perhaps Sadie hadn't been joking.

It was Tempest's turn to be exercised that day, so Martine rode the grey Arab colt while Ben tried to coax some life into Mambo. It wasn't an easy task. The pony had a fat stomach and a plump rump, and was both greedy and lazy. His nature was sweet enough, but he did everything in his own time and would not be hurried. Martine was sure that a charging elephant couldn't persuade Mambo to do anything more energetic than swish his tail.

'He's the perfect horse for a beginner,' Sadie told poor Ben, as it took the combined efforts of him and Ngwenya to drag the pony away from the feed trough.

Once they were on their way Mambo's behaviour improved, but the fastest he ever went was a trot. On this particular afternoon, that suited Martine and Ben fine, because Ben wanted to demonstrate some of the tracking skills he'd learned from Tendai. Sadie had lent them her binoculars and she asked them to report back if they saw any unusual birds or wildlife.

'Tendai says that anyone can learn the basic principles of tracking,' Ben told Martine as they rode across a plain about an hour away from the lodge. 'But the best trackers understand that it isn't just about reading "sign", which is things like broken twigs or whatever, but about trying to think like the animal or person you're following. It's a mind game. See this . . . ' He leaned down and pointed at some torn leaves lying in the long grass.

'These are crushed but they haven't wilted yet, which means that a large animal passed this way within the last hour or so. That's called 'sign' and it's obvious to an experienced tracker. The hard part comes if whatever you're following crosses an area where it leaves little or no trace, like a river or bare rock. That's when you have to use psychology. Tendai says that people crossing a stretch of water unconsciously walk in the direction they intend to travel, even if they're trying not to.'

Martine listened in admiration. Until a couple of years ago when his sailor father moved the family to Storm Crossing, Ben had grown up in one of Cape Town's roughest inner city areas. Dumisani Khumalo had taken his son fishing, or out on boats whenever he could, but before Martine had invited Ben to Sawubona he'd never had an opportunity to be close to wild animals or out in the bush. And yet to see him now anyone would think that he'd been having wilderness adventures all his life.

Martine supposed that in that way, at least, they were the same – kids from the suburbs, delivered by fate to Sawubona, where they'd fallen totally in love with nature. That's why they connected. That's why they understood each other. That's why Ben was her best friend.

The afternoon sun lit the top of the waving grasses so they shone blond against the blue sky. Ben stood in his stirrups, holding on to Mambo's shaggy white mane for balance. 'Hey, Martine, look over there. The way the shadows fall on the bent grass show us the path the animal has taken.'

Martine shaded her eyes and saw that he was right. A wiggly line of shadow gave away the creature's route across the plain as surely as if it had been advertised with neon lights. A little further on they found a heap of fresh dung. Ben identified it as being from a rhino.

'Rhino?' said Martine, pulling up Tempest. 'What's a rhino doing here? Didn't Sadie tell us that, snakes aside, there's nothing scarier than antelope on Black Eagle land?'

'She did,' agreed Ben, giving up his attempt to stop Mambo guzzling grass. 'A rhino shouldn't be here. That probably means it's either broken through a fence or walked through a fence that's been cut by poachers. We'd better follow it.'

Martine looked at him uncertainly. 'Ben, if we carry on past that *kopje*, we'll reach the northern boundary fence. Remember what Sadie said about us not going near it in case we're accidentally shot.' Ever since her row with Gwyn Thomas about riding Jemmy at night – a row that had gone unresolved for weeks because it happened hours before Martine left Sawubona for a school trip – she'd been trying very hard to do the right thing.

'Oh.' Ben was crestfallen.

Martine's resolve weakened. After a moment's hesitation, she continued, 'Mind you, we'd feel really bad if we went back without doing anything and the rhino was shot by mistake. We know we have to be careful if we're anywhere near the Lazy J, but the rhino doesn't.'

'I agree,' Ben said, 'but how are we going to keep it away from the boundary fence? Rhinos are incredibly lethal. We can't just herd it away as though we're rounding up a cow.'

Martine gathered up Tempest's reins. 'Let's stop when we reach the other side of the *kopje*, check out the situation with binoculars and decide what to do next. My grandmother will kill me if I end up getting shot.'

They both laughed at that. After a brief battle with Mambo, who was so determined to eat his fill of grass that Martine had to reattach his lead rope and tie it to the back of Tempest's saddle, they continued on their way.

As soon as they rounded the *kopje*, they spotted the rhino. It was grazing under a tree. Luckily the wind direction was in their favour and rhino have poor eyesight, so it didn't notice them. It did, however, notice the sharp crack that suddenly split the air. Its horn jerked up and its piggy eyes swivelled as it tried to assess the threat. It didn't hang around for long. With astonishing speed, it tore around the *kopje* and out of view.

The combination of the rifle shot and the rhino's hasty exit was too much for Tempest, who bolted a few strides before being brought up short by Mambo's lead rope. He reared in panic. Martine had to use all her giraffe-riding experience to cling on and soothe him. If Ben's pony hadn't stayed relatively placid throughout, disaster would have quickly followed.

'What was that?' Martine demanded when she'd finally managed to settle the Arab. 'I know it was a gun shot, but who fired it? Were they trying to hit the rhino?'

Ben put the binoculars to his eyes. 'I don't think so,' he said. 'It looks like there's something going on at the Lazy J, but it's hard to make out what at this distance. There are a lot of people gathered around a sort of paddock enclosed by a high fence. Let's go a bit closer.'

They rode until they were practically touching the boundary fence that divided Black Eagle from the Lazy J. Martine felt guilty about going against Sadie's wishes, but she was as determined as Ben not to leave until they knew what had happened at the hunting lodge.

Ben lifted the glasses again. 'There's a man entering the enclosure on his own. He's wearing a hat and a khaki safari suit and he has a really big stomach. It's huge. He looks pregnant. He's holding something in his hand but I can't see what it is. Either a stick or a gun.'

'Let me look,' said Martine, reaching for the binoculars.

Ben held them out of range. 'Hold on a second. A small gate is opening in the wall and . . . Oh, wow. A male lion has come out. Martine, he's so beautiful. He has the most amazing dark mane and he's a tawny colour with big muscles.'

'Ben, please!' Martine begged, but before she could say anything else another shot rang out.

Ben's body went rigid. The colour fled from his face and an expression of absolute horror came over it.

'What is it, Ben?' cried Martine. 'What have you seen? Has something happened to the lion?'

'It's nothing,' he mumbled. 'Martine, let's get away from here. The Lazy J is a wicked place.' He looked as if he was about to cry. 'Come on, Mambo, let's go.'

Martine took advantage of his struggles with the pony to snatch the binoculars, which he'd hooked around the pommel of his saddle.

'No, Martine, don't!' yelled Ben.

But Martine had already wheeled Tempest and was lifting the glasses to her eyes. The lion lay dead on the ground. The hunter had one foot on its chest and one hand on his rifle and he was smiling and posing for photographs. The lion's blood was leaking out onto his boot, but he didn't seem to notice.

Tears started to pour down Martine's face. She put down the glasses, buried her head in Tempest's mane and sobbed uncontrollably. She wept for the proud lion, cut down without a chance so that a fat man could have a lion-skin rug in his home and a bloody photograph on his wall. She wept for the white giraffe whom she missed and who was safe at Sawubona when he, too, could so easily have lost his life to hunters. She wept for all the other animals whose fate it was to die alone and unloved at the hands of cruel, selfish human beings.

And gradually she became aware that Ben – the bravest boy she knew – was crying for exactly the same reasons.

That evening the sun, slipping below the ragged green hills, was the colour of blood, and as they rode home through the lengthening black shadows the rocks moaned just as Ngwenya had described, only it was not the voice of Mwali that Martine heard, but the cries of all the animals who would go helplessly to their graves at the Lazy J unless she and Ben did something to prevent it.

9

'Canned Hunting,' Sadie said heavily. 'That's what it's called.'

They'd confronted her soon after returning to Black Eagle, their faces dusty and streaked with tears. She and Martine's grandmother had come rushing to meet them at the stables, ready to scold them for returning so late, but Sadie had taken one look at them and dispatched Gwyn Thomas, protesting loudly, to deal with dinner. Ngwenya wouldn't hear of them feeding or rubbing down their horses. They'd ended up sitting outside the stables with Sadie who'd listened without saying anything to their passionate account of the horror they'd witnessed at the Lazy J.

Now they were gathered around the kitchen table in the flickering candlelight. It was spring in Southern Africa and the temperature still dropped steeply at night so there was a crackling fire burning in the grate. Under any other circumstances, Martine thought, the scene would have been magical.

Gwyn Thomas said, 'What is canned hunting?'

'It's when animals which are dangerous, rare, or hard to track, such as lion, leopard or rhino, are put into small enclosures in order for hunters to safely and easily shoot them,' Sadie explained. 'These hunters are usually rich tourists or powerful men like government ministers who want a guaranteed kill with minimum risk. They want to go home with a skin or a horn or a couple of tusks, and tell stories about how they stalked and shot a deadly wild animal.

'Rex Ratcliffe, who owns the Lazy J, has always claimed that he is running a respectable safari and hunting operation, but Ngwenya and I have suspected for many years that he is up to all sorts of tricks, including canned hunting. What you've seen today proves it. I'm sorry you had to witness that. I hope you can put it behind you and enjoy the rest of your stay at Black Eagle.' She reached for a serving plate. 'Anyone for butternut fritters?'

Martine couldn't believe her ears. Sadie had as good as told them that her next-door neighbour was murdering wildlife in cold blood. She couldn't seriously expect them to continue their holiday without a care.

As for the fritters, well, Martine liked butternut squash as much as anyone, but after almost a week of eating it for breakfast, lunch and dinner, she was heartily tired of it. She found it peculiar that the groceries they'd brought had gone into the locked pantry and never come out again, but suspected that if times were as hard at Black Eagle as they appeared to be, Sadie was probably saving the interesting food for any visitors who might show up. Not that it mattered this evening. Every time her stomach rumbled Martine remembered the lion and felt sick again.

'You must eat something,' urged her grandmother. 'Have some potatoes or even just a slice of bread and peanut butter.'

Martine took a few potatoes to keep Gwyn Thomas happy but did little more than move them round her plate. Across the table, Ben was doing the same.

Sadie seemed determined to ensure there was no more talk of hunting or dead lions. She launched into a dreary rant about the high price of spare parts for cars. Martine started to simmer. She was fed up with Sadie pretending that everything at Black Eagle was completely fine when it obviously wasn't. The fire was making her very hot and that didn't help her mood either.

Ben seemed to guess what she was about to do and gave a warning shake of his head. When she ignored him, he kicked her under the table. Martine took no notice. She waited until Sadie paused for breath and said, 'Why are you being blackmailed?'

Sadie's fork paused on the way to her mouth. Her

fingers lost coordination and she dropped it with a clatter.

'Martine!' her grandmother said angrily. 'Have you taken complete leave of your senses? What on earth are you talking about? Apologize to Sadie at once.'

Sadie was staring at Martine. 'What did you say?'

'It *is* blackmail, isn't it?' Martine demanded, risking her grandmother's wrath. 'Whose blood money don't you want? Who are you trying to hold on to? Is it Ngwenya?'

Gwyn Thomas jumped to her feet. 'This is outrageous. I've heard more than enough. Martine, go to bed at once and we'll talk about this in the morning. I'm so sorry, Sadie. I've no idea what's got into her.'

Sadie stopped her. 'Sit down, Gwyn,' she ordered. 'You too, Martine. You've done nothing wrong. Quite the reverse. Ever since I telephoned you at Sawubona and asked you to come here, I've been wracked with guilt. I felt I was deceiving you all, asking you to come here and not telling you what you might be letting yourselves in for. But I was desperate. When I broke my leg, I had no one else to turn to. No one else I trusted enough to ask, at any rate. Ngwenya has been wonderful, but he has a family to go home to at night. I guess I was afraid.'

Gwyn Thomas seemed unsure whether to be curious or furious. 'But who are you afraid of? Are there bandits around here? Poachers?'

'No,' responded Sadie. 'At least, yes, of course there are, but it's not them that I'm afraid of. I'm not really afraid of anyone. I'm afraid *for* someone . . . Well, not someone as such . . .'

Gwyn Thomas sat back in her chair. 'Now I'm really confused.'

Sadie sighed. 'Let's make a strong coffee,' she said. 'I think I need to explain from the beginning.'

It all started when Sadie's father, Colonel Scott, agreed to rehabilitate a young leopard into the wild on Black Eagle land on behalf of a famous Bulawayo wildlife orphanage, Chipangali. The project was an instant success. The leopard, a male named Khan after the Indian doctor who'd found him as a week-old cub, orphaned by a bushfire, took to the Matobo Hills as if he'd been in the wilderness all his life.

'You told us that you'd only seen him once,' Martine reminded Sadie. 'It must have been more often than that if your father was rehabilitating him.'

Sadie gave a small smile. 'No, I was telling you the truth about that. I saw Khan the day he came to Black Eagle, but the following day I had to leave for South Africa for a hotel management course I was booked on. When I returned Khan had already made his home in the bush and was as elusive as any other leopard.

'At the time of my father's death a little over a year ago, our main feeling regarding the leopard was pride, I suppose. Animals belong in the wild, not behind bars

79

like prisoners, and we were proud that we'd been able to give Khan his freedom. Our problems started when I began to get reports of his immense size from the few people who glimpsed him. Male leopards have a territory of up to forty kilometres square. I'd hear tales of his magnificence from far and wide. Once he was grown, he no longer stayed exclusively on Black Eagle property.

'Four months ago, I was approached by Rex Ratcliffe. He offered me several thousand pounds in foreign currency if I would sell him Khan for use in one of his 'safaris'. I was sure that he really wanted him for canned hunting, but in any case I said that Khan was not mine to sell. He was free and that was the way he was going to stay. I told Ratcliffe that if I ever caught him or any of his hunters near my land, I'd shoot him myself.'

Martine was on the edge of her seat. 'Go on,' she encouraged as Sadie stoked the fire with the tip of one of her crutches.

'Khan was only ever seen in two areas – Black Eagle and the Matobo National Park. Since the wildlife in the national park is protected, Ratcliffe focussed his efforts on Black Eagle. He began to blackmail me. He did it in ways so subtle that I could never prove he was behind it, but it was obvious. Tour operators started calling me to say they'd heard rats had been found in Black Eagle kitchens. Rumours circulated of thieving staff and dirty rooms. Within weeks, my business had all but dried up at the retreat. To add to our problems, five of our cattle died mysteriously, probably from poisoning, and one of our main waterholes was contaminated. Plus the guards on the national park gate gave me trouble when I travelled to and from Bulawayo. I held out for as long as I could, but last month I was forced to lay off most of my staff. Then, of course, I broke my leg slipping on a greasy substance that had been left on my doorstep, and had to call you.'

'Did you contact the police?' asked Gwyn Thomas.

'What could I say? There's absolutely no evidence to connect Ratcliffe or the Lazy J to what's going on.'

'What about the phone call?' Ben suggested. 'There'll be phone records. You could tell the police that he's been threatening you.'

Sadie gave a dry laugh. 'Rex Ratcliffe's much too smart for that. He uses an unlisted number, which means that no number appears on the telephone bill. And he's very careful to be polite and not use threats. He always calls a couple of days after something bad has happened, such as the poisoning of the cattle, and offers me more and more money for Khan. He talks to me as if I'm senile and too simple to know what I'm turning down. He says things like, "Think about it. It's not as if Black Eagle's doing very well these days, is it now, Sadie?"

'"The Rat", as I call him, partly because he bears a remarkable resemblance to a rodent, believes everyone has a price. He doesn't understand what it is to love a person or animal so much that you would lay down your life for them.'

She looked around sheepishly. 'You don't think I'm senile as well, do you?'

'I don't,' Martine told her. 'I can totally understand what it's like to love an animal so much you'd do anything for them. That's how I feel about Jemmy, my white giraffe. He's—'

'Let's have no more talk of laying down lives,' interrupted her grandmother. 'Let's talk about solutions. However, I'm upset with you, Sadie, for not telling me this before we came. I'm responsible for Martine and Ben and it was unfair of you not to inform me what was going on so that I could use my judgement about whether or not it was safe to bring them.'

'I'm sorry,' Sadie mumbled. 'I know I did the wrong thing. But I was sure that if you knew the truth you wouldn't come.'

'Having said that,' Gwyn Thomas went on, 'I can appreciate what an ordeal this must have been for you, and since we are here I think I speak for Martine and Ben when I say that we'll do everything we can to help you keep Black Eagle Lodge and protect Khan. We just have to figure out how.'

Martine and Ben voiced their enthusiastic agreement, and Martine was very proud of her grandmother for caring so much about helping her friend and saving the leopard that she was willing to overlook Sadie's deception. Still, she couldn't help thinking back to Ngwenya's words about the treasure seekers' quest: 'In order to find the treasure, the leopard first has to be dead.'

That meant they were up against two groups of potential leopard assassins: Ngwenya's cousin and his gold-digging *shamwaris*, whom she and Ben had promised Ngwenya they wouldn't speak about, and Rex Ratcliffe and goodness knows how many hunters from the Lazy J.

'Thank you all for your kindness,' Sadie said, her eyes shiny in the firelight. 'You've no idea how much it means to me. But I have to be honest with you. We have a fight on our hands and I want you to be under no illusions about how difficult that fight will be. The Rat and his hunters want the leopard. They want Khan. And they won't stop until they get him.'

10

Martine was being buried alive. Moist, cool earth – earth that smelled of worms and rotting leaves – was filling her mouth and eyes and ears, and as fast as she tried to spit it out or push it away from her, more came in. She tried to scream, but no sound came out of her mouth. She tried to run, but her legs wouldn't work.

'Martine. Martine, wake up.'

Martine sat up in bed, gulping for oxygen, relieved when no sand or worms came with it. Her eyes adjusted to the darkness. Ben was standing in front of the window, his small, strong frame backlit by a sky of glittering stars. He was fully dressed.

'Hey, I didn't mean to scare you,' he whispered. 'Were you having a nightmare or something? Are you all right?'

Martine rubbed the sleep from her eyes. 'What time is it?'

'It's a little after four a.m. I know it's awfully early but I can't sleep. I keep thinking about Khan. I feel like we need to find him. How can we protect him when we don't even know where he is?'

Instantly Martine was alert. 'You're right. We have to find him so we can figure out a way to save him. But what are we going to tell Sadie and my grandmother? Somehow I don't think they'll agree to us going in search of one of the world's biggest leopards in pitch darkness, even if we are trying to help him.'

'We'll leave a note telling them we've gone on an early morning ride,' said Ben. 'Which is true. We *are* going on an early morning ride. It's just that it'll be a few hours earlier than usual, and we'll be keeping an eye out for a leopard at the same time.'

Put like that the plan sounded perfectly reasonable, so Martine hopped out of bed and put on her jeans, boots, and a sweatshirt while Ben went to write a note for Sadie and Gwyn Thomas. On the way out of the cottage, they filled their pockets with buttermilk rusks, the only treat that hadn't disappeared into Sadie's locked pantry. As they hadn't touched their dinner the previous night, they were ravenously hungry.

The hornbill was the only one to see them go. He followed them to the stables and watched with his head cocked as they saddled the horses by torchlight.

'Don't you ever get any sleep, Magnus?' Martine asked the bird, jumping to intercept him as he hopped slyly towards her shimmering pink Maglite on the stable floor. 'And I've told you before, keep your claws off my stuff.'

They took the path around Elephant Rock, keeping to the grassy edges so that the horses' hooves were muffled. 'Shhh, Sirocco,' said Martine as the Arab gave a series of loud sneezes and jingled her bit in the process. Ben was riding Cassidy and Martine was leading Jack.

They were at the gates of Ngwenya's village in under ten minutes. The silhouettes of the hut roofs looked like pyramids under the night sky. They tied up the horses and entered through the main gate. The smell of sadza – the maize meal porridge that is the staple food of Zimbabweans – hung in the air, mingled with the smoky smell of old fires. A sleeping dog roused itself and gave a few feeble barks, but Ben stroked it and it quietened.

Ngwenya had pointed out his home when they'd been riding one day, so they had no trouble locating it. They knocked on his door and he stumbled out blinking.

'What are you doing here?' he said in alarm. 'Do Gogo and Mrs Thomas know you are here? Is there trouble at the house?'

Ben assured him that everything was fine and briefly filled him in on the events of the previous afternoon and evening, which he hadn't heard because he'd been tending to the horses.

'So you see, we have to find the leopard,' Martine said

eagerly. 'We can't protect him if we don't know where he is. Only we need your help because we wouldn't even know where to start. Especially in the dark.'

Ngwenya gave a snort of laughter. 'Do you know how difficult it is to find this leopard? I myself have never seen him. There are many, many caves and tunnels and hiding places in these hills. It is impossible. Go back to sleep and at breakfast you can speak to Gogo.'

Martine tried not to let her irritation show. 'But you must have some idea where he is,' she persisted. 'From time to time people must have mentioned to you that they've glimpsed him on this hill or that one. We could start by going to the last place anyone saw him. He might not be there any more, but maybe Ben could track him to his new den.'

'Hayikona,' Ngwenya said stubbornly. 'No. Gogo and Mrs Thomas will be too angry with me. First you must speak with them. This is not a cat from your house you are looking for. This is a leopard which can kill you with one paw.'

'This is also a leopard that the hunters can kill with one bullet if we don't stop them,' Martine pointed out.

Ngwenya went back into his hut without another word and slammed the door.

'We're wasting our time,' said Ben. 'He's not going to change his mind.'

Martine put her mouth close to the clay wall of the hut. 'What about your cousin?' she said loudly. 'I thought it was your clan oath to protect the leopard. Does anyone else in the clan know that your cousin and his friends want the leopard dead so they can get their hands on Lobengula's treasure?'

The hut door flew open. 'Please,' implored Ngwenya. 'You must not speak of these things. There are people in this village who are not of our clan.'

'Then will you help us?'

He stared at her in exasperation. 'I don't know where to find him,' he said. 'There are only rumours, stories. Nobody knows for sure.'

Martine's gaze was unflinching. 'You know in your heart where he is.'

Ngwenya dropped his eyes. It was plain that he was wrestling with his conscience. Finally he came to a decision. 'Wait,' he said, 'I will get my shoes and my rifle.'

The sheer rock was rough and warm beneath Martine's fingertips. Thanks to the long hours spent on horseback, time she wasn't able to spend riding the white giraffe during term time, she was much fitter than she had been when she first arrived at Black Eagle. But it was still a stiff climb up a seemingly endless granite mountain.

At the very top was a cave. Unlike the Memory Room in the Secret Valley, this one was open to the air and formed of a rock so pale it was almost white. In the fading blue of the departing night, it was visible from quite a distance. A pillar-shaped boulder stood like a sentinel at its entrance, which was perfectly round. As they approached, they could see the cave was decorated with vivid Bushmen paintings and that there was a narrow tunnel tucked away in the back.

'This is the last place that the leopard was seen,' Ngwenya said, gesturing with the rifle he'd brought in case of an emergency. 'But it is many weeks since I heard this.'

'Martine, Ngwenya and I will go down the tunnel to see if we can find any trace of him,' Ben said. 'It's too dangerous for all three of us to go at once. You keep a look out.'

'No!' Martine cried in panic. 'We can't be separated. Remember Grace's warning.'

'Don't worry,' Ben said. 'We won't be gone long and we won't be far away. If you need us, yell, and we'll come running.'

Ngwenya agreed. 'It's much safer for you here. If the leopard is in his den, we will be exiting as fast as cheetahs. Two will be quicker than three.'

'And we need someone on guard,' Ben added. 'If the leopard is out hunting and comes back when we're inside the cave, it'll be a disaster.'

Martine wasn't at all happy about being left alone, but she didn't want them to think she was a coward either. And it was important that someone kept watch.

After they'd gone, she tried to take her mind off her fears by being a good security guard and keeping a very close eye on the valley below. In the few minutes since their arrival, a blush of orange had crept above the horizon. Dawn was on its way. Martine started to feel better. There was something about the rising of the sun that helped chase away the lingering anxiety caused by her nightmare.

She took off her sweatshirt and tossed it onto a nearby rock, and a cool breeze brushed her skin. All around her the hills of the Matopos unfurled in lumpy folds of green and brown. Boulders like domes and spires and beasts and birds perched, reared or leaned precariously. As far as Martine could tell, the only things moving in the shadowed valley below were the horses tethered at the bottom of the mountain. A lone *dassie*, a favourite food of leopards, sniffed along the base of the cave until it saw it had company and darted away.

As it grew lighter, Martine went over to examine the paintings. She never tired of looking at cave pictures, finding them endlessly fascinating and thrilling, and the sketches here were especially well-preserved. Their dusky pink, grey and ochre colours had survived thousands of years with barely a blemish. There were the usual scenes of hunts, feasts and ceremonies, but she was surprised to find that there were quite a lot of similarities between these pictures and those in the Memory Room cave at Sawubona, almost as if they were the work of the same artist. She supposed that the painting techniques of the San had been handed down through the generations.

One image was set slightly apart. Martine wandered over to take a look at it. It showed a girl standing at the entrance to a cave – the cave Martine was in now, if its round mouth and sentinel-like pillar were anything to go by. And crouched on the pillar, as if it were about to pounce, was a leopard – the leopard she'd seen in the sand.

Martine froze. What if *she* was the girl in the picture? What if the leopard . . . ?

But she knew the answer even before she'd finished the thought.

She smelt him before she saw him. It wasn't an unpleasant smell – if anything, there was something wonderful about it. It was the scent of a wild, free thing. But it was also the smell of a killer.

At Sawubona, Martine had rehearsed this moment a hundred times in case she was ever confronted by a predator when out riding Jemmy. But in her imagination she'd always been able to gallop away on the white giraffe. Now she was alone.

She dragged her eyes upwards. The leopard was on the ledge above her, regal both in stature and in size. His creamy gold coat had the rich sheen of the finest silk, his black spots gleamed, and his yellow eyes blazed like topaz fires. She had always admired leopards in photographs, always yearned to see an adult one in real life. Her glimpse of the rescued leopard cubs at Sawubona had been brief because Tendai had been anxious to return them to their mother. But nothing could have prepared her for the unquenchable spirit of Khan in the flesh. Power and wildness radiated from him.

With one bound, he smashed her to the earth. His great paws thudded against her chest and his claws pierced her skin, and then she was on the ground, winded and in pain. She could feel blood trickling down her armpit.

Khan stood over her, his huge paws on either side of her body. The look in his eyes was one of undiluted fury and hatred. She knew he'd kill her without a care. He gave a savage snarl and his whiskered lips curled back over pink gums. His teeth were so close to her throat that Martine could feel his hot breath on her face.

'Yell and we'll come running,' Ben had promised, but she'd be dead long before he could get to her and Khan would probably die too, because in spite of his clan oath Ngwenya wouldn't hesitate to shoot the leopard to try to save her.

Twice in the past, Martine's gift had allowed her to halt a deadly attack: once when a rottweiller dog had tried to stop her from rescuing Jemmy, and another time when a Great White shark was on the verge of eating an American tourist. But that had required concentration and a supreme effort of will, and now she was so frightened she was incapable of summoning either of those things. She lay on the ground like a blob of jelly. And yet she couldn't hate the leopard for what he was about to do to her. There were very good reasons for his loathing of humans. She understood that he was afraid himself.

But there was something else in his yellow eyes, something besides hatred and fear. There was a sadness and tiredness that seemed bone-deep, as if he was exhausted by the endless struggle to survive. And it was those things that made Martine realize that, even without knowing him, she cared for him. She felt the same pure love for the leopard she'd felt for Jemmy on the night they'd first met.

'Please don't hurt me,' she said to Khan. 'All I want to do is help you.'

The leopard roared. She recognized it as the defiant, rage-filled sound she'd heard on the first night at Black Eagle. At close quarters, it was bloodcurdling.

There was a drumbeat echo of footsteps as Ben and Ngwenya returned at speed. Martine wasn't sure which she feared most – that Khan would maul her before they could reach her, or that they'd reach her in time but shoot him to save her. She was about to close her eyes and pray that the end, whether it was the leopard's or her own, was quick, when some of the wildness seemed to leave Khan. He gave her a last, unfathomable look before melting away into the bush. Martine scrambled to her feet and dusted herself off.

Ben burst out of the tunnel mouth first. 'Martine! Martine! Oh, thank God you're okay. Did you hear that roar? It nearly frightened the life out of us. We should never have left you. I don't know what I was thinking. It just seemed the safest thing to do.'

He suddenly became aware that Martine wasn't saying anything. Then he noticed the red specks on her T-shirt. 'Is that blood?'

It was on the tip of Martine's tongue to tell him about Khan, but then Ngwenya came rushing over and wanted them to leave right away in case Khan was still in the vicinity, and Martine realized that there was no way of putting into words what had just taken place.

How could she say that the leopard which had eluded rangers who'd worked in the Matopos for twenty years had knocked her to the ground and stood over her with the clear intention of killing her, but that something had passed between them – an understanding – and at the last conceivable second he'd changed his mind.

How could she explain that she'd looked into his blazing yellow eyes and seen beyond the hatred to the weary sadness of a creature hunted almost every day of his existence? How could she explain that without even knowing him, she loved him?

'I'm fine,' she replied. 'I slipped on a rock, that's all. I did hear the roar and I was a bit scared, but I knew you were close by. I knew you'd come running if I needed you, and you did.'

11

They rode back through the honeyed light of the breaking morning, munching on rusks. All three of them were lost in thought. Martine was thinking about Khan, and if and when she'd ever see him again. She was determined to do everything in her power to protect him from Rex Ratcliffe's evil hunters.

Ben was thinking about Cassidy, who never seemed to go where she was meant to go, and he was thinking about Martine. He was positive she'd seen the leopard, and not only seen him, but been clawed by him. But far from being upset that she hadn't admitted it, her silence on the subject made him admire her even more.

Ben couldn't stand vain or boastful people. He knew perfectly well that, with the exception of Martine, there was not one kid in Caracal Junior School who could have survived an encounter with the largest wild leopard ever recorded and not gloated about it forever and wanted to see themselves on the evening news.

Martine was the opposite of them. She'd done what she thought was best for Khan. He watched her guide Sirocco skilfully over a narrow stream and up the bank on the other side and grinned to himself. He couldn't have wished for a better best friend.

Ngwenya, meanwhile, was feeling like a failure. Ever since Khan's release into the wild at Black Eagle he'd vowed to do whatever was necessary to keep the leopard out of the hands of hunters and poachers, but it had taken two children who were not even from the Matopos to spur him into action and point out the most obvious thing: how can you save the leopard if you don't even know where he is?

Ngwenya had helped Colonel Scott set Khan free, and it had been clear to him even then that this was no ordinary leopard. Khan's paws had been the size of baseball mitts. Ngwenya was desperately disappointed to have been so close to the leopard again and yet miss him. Like Ben, he was certain that Martine had seen the leopard. It seemed to have scratched her. It was puzzling that she'd not breathed a word about it and was now riding her horse quite contentedly as if being clawed by leopards was an everyday event for her.

There was no doubt that she was a most unusual

child. She looked perfectly ordinary with her cropped brown hair, green eyes and skinny limbs, but he'd noticed that Magnus and the horses had formed very strong attachments to her. Then there was this business of her riding a giraffe. Clearly there was much more to her than met the eye.

It was almost eight a.m. when the trio rounded Elephant Rock, riding three abreast. The first thing they saw was a blue-and-white-striped car in the retreat driveway, visible through the gum trees. Ngwenya suddenly yanked at Martine and Ben's bridles, pulling up their horses with a start.

'The police,' he whispered. He put a finger to his lips and dismounted rapidly, indicating that they should do the same.

'The police?' cried Martine, forgetting to keep her voice down. 'Then what are we waiting for?' She sprang off her horse. 'I'm going to run and see what's going on. My grandmother or Sadie might have had an accident. There could have been a robbery. Anything could have happened.'

'No!' Ngwenya snatched her back roughly. 'In this country, the police can be more dangerous than the criminals. Maybe they are on a routine patrol or maybe they have been called by Gogo and your grandmother, but we must approach with caution.'

They led the horses back the way they came and tied them up beneath an overhang screened by trees. Then they crept round the back of the stables and through the gum trees until they were within spitting distance of the police car. A low stone wall provided them with cover. Nothing happened for a few minutes and then Sadie and Gwyn Thomas emerged from the house with two policemen. Martine gasped. Her grandmother was in handcuffs and Sadie was remonstrating with a young constable who was gripping her arm as she swung along on crutches.

'I'm not going to deny I told Mr Rat that I'd shoot him and his hunters if they set foot on my land . . . ' she was saying unrepentantly.

'Mr Rat*cliffe*,' corrected the constable. 'His name is Mr Ratcliffe.'

Sadie frowned. 'Whatever. I'd tell him the same thing again. But that's a very different thing from actually doing it – shooting him, that is. Mr Rat is still alive, isn't he?'

'Sadie,' interjected Gwyn Thomas, appalled, 'I think the less said the better, don't you? Let's cooperate with these nice policeman and go down to the station and I'm sure we'll have it all sorted out in no time.'

'Why you want to kill Mr Rat— er, Mr Ratcliffe?' demanded the other policeman. 'Are you jealous that his business is doing well and Black Eagle Lodge is in some difficulty?'

'Don't be ridiculous,' snapped Sadie. 'How can I be jealous of a man whose business is murdering animals? And besides, if Black Eagle is in difficulty it's because Mr Rat has driven away all my customers. It's him you should be arresting, not me, and certainly not my friend who has done absolutely nothing.'

'Sadie,' cried Gwyn Thomas, 'not another word. Do you want them to lock us up and throw away the key? Officer, can you read us our rights?'

The young constable looked bemused to be asked to do his job. Behind the wall, Ngwenya and the children were struggling to take in this bizarre turn of events. 'You have the right to remain silent,' the constable parroted dutifully. 'Anything you say can and will be held against you ... '

'Wait,' said the other policeman. 'Where is the man who usually works with you? Ngwenya, is it? Also, Mr Ratcliffe mentioned some children.'

Fear flitted across Gwyn Thomas's face.

'How did he ... ?' Sadie began. 'Never mind. Yes, you are quite correct, Mrs Thomas's granddaughter and a boy, Ben, were here, but you know how children are these days – in constant need of entertainment. They were bored in the bush with nothing to do. They missed television or video games or something. I had Ngwenya take them to Bulawayo to stay with some friends of mine for three or four days. He had some business in the city. He was going to spend time there and bring them back towards the end of the week.'

'Kids, they are very expensive,' agreed the young constable moodily. 'All the time my son is wanting new shoes, new clothes, new CDs, new books for school. And he is always eating. I tell him ... '

'Shut up, Shepherd,' said the surly policeman. 'You talk too much. Let's take these women down to the station.'

The officers were marching their unlikely prisoners to

the car when Magnus flew down from the trees and landed on the wall. He hopped along the chestnut bricks until he was close to Martine, and then cocked his head and opened his beak as if he was about to start chatting to her.

From her crouching position, Martine tried to wave him away before he drew attention to them. Ngwenya even prodded him with a stick. But the hornbill just hopped out of range.

'What is that funny bird doing?' enquired the policeman, locking Gwyn Thomas in the back of the car and striding in their direction.

Through a hole in the wall, Martine saw it dawn on Sadie why Magnus was behaving so oddly. 'I wouldn't go too near if I were you,' she cautioned the policeman. 'You've heard about the deadly bird flu which kills human beings within twenty-four hours? Well, it's been proven that hornbills are particularly likely to get it. That hornbill has been sneezing for days.'

Magnus chose that very second to swoop off the wall and make a lunge for the keys that dangled, gleaming, from the policeman's belt.

The policeman screamed like a girl. 'Get away, sick bird,' he squawked, flapping his arms. 'Get away!' He dived into the car and turned on the ignition.

Sadie took advantage of the distraction to say loudly, 'I'm really glad that the children aren't here, because if they were they'd be worried about us and there's really no reason to be. This is a ridiculous misunderstanding. We'll be back by lunchtime, I'm sure. But whatever happens, it's nice to know that they'll be safe with Ngwenya. He'll take care of them.'

'Why are you shouting when I am right here?' barked the constable. He bundled her into the back seat, tossing her crutches in after her. 'Get a move on. You are making us late.'

The police car departed in a crunch of gravel. The engine faded and the blanketing silence descended once more.

Martine felt ill. Usually it was her grandmother who worried about her. Now it was the other way round.

'What do we do now?' Ben said.

Ngwenya's face was grim. 'We make a plan.'

'Don't you bring trouble to our door.'

The speaker was Ngwenya's uncle's wife, Mercy. She stood with her arms folded like a bodyguard, glowering at the horse wrangler. A baby was strapped to her back with a towel. Her husband, a wiry man a third of her size with the mournful expression of a bloodhound, trembled slightly at her side. His eyes never left the ground, although from time to time he stooped to pet two mongrels.

Mercy jerked her chin towards Martine and Ben, whom she hadn't even greeted. 'My baby is not well. She has been crying all day. We have many problems and now you ask us to hide the children of a grandmother wanted by the police. Ha! You are very irresponsible, Ngwenya.'

Martine thought it might be the wrong moment to inform her that a) Gwyn Thomas was not wanted by the police but had been wrongfully arrested; and b) Ben was not her half-brother.

Mercy shook her head in disgust. 'You are very irresponsible, Ngwenya,' she said again. 'Do you think we want trouble coming to our house? Do you think we need the police at our door?'

Ngwenya threw an anguished glance at Martine and Ben. 'Mercy, please,' he begged. 'These are two innocent children. Gogo and Martine's grandmother are also innocent. They need our help. I cannot keep them in my own village because it is too near to the retreat. You would not want somebody to turn away baby Emelia if she is ever in need of sanctuary when she is older. It is not their fault this has happened. It is the fault of Mr Ratcliffe.'

Mercy said sharply, 'Mr Ratcliffe? What has Mr Rat been doing now?'

'He is the reason that Black Eagle Lodge is going out of business,' Ngwenya told her. 'He is the reason that Gogo has had to lay off most of her staff. I have not spoken of this to anyone because I promised her I would not, but he has made her life hell by starting rumours about thieving employees and dirty rooms. He has poisoned our cattle and threatened Gogo. We can't prove it, but we know he is behind these things. It is blackmail.'

Mercy was briefly dumbstruck. 'But why? What reason would he have to make his neighbour suffer like this?'

'He wants the leopard. Gogo would not allow him to buy Khan so that he or his hunters could kill him, and he is not a man who understands the word no. She warned him she would shoot him if he came on our land, and he sent the police to arrest her. They have taken Martine's grandmother for no reason.'

Mercy addressed Martine and Ben for the first time. 'This man Rat cost my husband his job,' she said. 'Odilo, my husband, was a proud man, but Mr Ratcliffe has friends in the government and together they shut down the mine where Odilo worked because it was close to the edge of Mr Ratcliffe's land. Now Odilo has a lot of sadness and life is not easy for us. There is little money. But an enemy of Mr Ratcliffe is a friend to us. You will stay here, of course. Please, sit down for a cup of tea.'

Martine was worried sick about her grandmother, but she found the experience of being in an African village fascinating. The huts had thatched roofs like inverted ice-cream cones, and their clay walls were prettily decorated. They were insulated with cow dung to keep them cool during the day and warm at night. Inside, mattresses with woven quilts were placed on platforms of bricks, raised to keep the sleeper safe from the dwarf spirit Tokoloshe, who, Mercy told them, kidnapped his victims and took them down to his watery den. Everything had the faint smell of woodsmoke.

Chickens pecked around the outdoor cooking area, where two women were pounding maize into the meal used to make sadza porridge. The village was set on the edge of a large, flat plain, across which could be seen the low grey buildings of a school. Behind Martine and Ben's temporary home, a red-brown hut with zigzag patterns, was a circle of low *kopjes*, shaggy with shrubs and trees. The hills formed a natural paddock with only one exit. Mambo, Sirocco and Red Mist were in there grazing with the cattle and sheep. Ngwenya was planning to return to Black Eagle for the night so that he could keep an eye on the retreat and take care of the other horses.

Apart from the rhythmic thud of the *mielie* crushers, the village was quiet, so quiet that any approaching police car would be heard for miles.

'Don't be frightened for Sadie and Mrs Thomas,' Ngwenya counselled Ben and Martine. 'They've done nothing wrong and will be home very soon. Not even Mr Ratcliffe can make the police lock away innocent people for more than one or two days. They are just going to question them and release them – maybe even by this afternoon.'

The thing that bothered Martine was what would happen if her grandmother and Sadie didn't return to Black Eagle in a matter of days. She and Ben could hardly ride their horses through the streets of Bulawayo, like characters out of a cowboy film, and demand that the women were freed. An unfamiliar feeling of powerlessness had come over her as Gwyn Thomas was driven away.

Ever since she'd returned from the island, she and her grandmother had grown closer and closer. For the first six months after her parents died, a little part of Martine had kept expecting to wake up and find that the fire had been a hideous nightmare and they weren't really dead after all. She'd kept thinking that at any second her mum would walk through the door, or her dad would grab her around the waist and tickle her until she cried with laughter. But at a certain point, a little over a month ago, she'd realized that it was never going to happen. She was never going to see her parents again. It was then that her grandmother, Jemmy and Ben had become the centre of her world. She depended on them utterly. And now two of those loved ones were far away and she didn't know when, or if, they'd all be reunited.

Ben read her thoughts. He was very concerned about how long it would be before he saw his own parents again, and more than a little worried about what he and Martine had got themselves into in pursuing the leopard, but he was determined to be strong for Martine's sake. He said, 'There's no point in dwelling on what we can't do. Let's figure out what we can do.'

'I don't know what that is,' Martine burst out. 'I don't know where to begin.'

'Why don't we start with the Lazy J?' Ben suggested.

That evening, the aroma of chicken sizzling over the coals and the nutty smell of bubbling sadza filled the air. Mouths watering, Martine and Ben warmed themselves beside the fire as the villagers buzzed around them, cooking, chopping, preparing. Martine could imagine that on most nights a relaxed, sociable atmosphere of community and friendship would prevail in the village, but tonight there was tension in the faces of the men, women and even children. Mercy's baby had a fever and was now desperately ill. Odilo had sent for the witchdoctor.

When the baby finally fell asleep, Mercy joined them

for the meal, although Martine noticed that she barely touched her food.

'How is Emelia?' enquired Ngwenya.

Mercy's expression told him all he needed to know. 'I would feel much better if I knew we didn't have to depend on the witchdoctor,' she said. 'He is the best we have, but he has a weakness for . . . '

She trailed off in mid-sentence. 'Let us hope that he has had a good day.'

Martine and Ben followed the lead of Ngwenya who, like everyone else, ate with his hands, rolling the sadza into snowy balls which he used to scoop up chicken pieces and a spicy relish of spinach and tomato. He and Odilo were interested in Sawubona and asked lots of questions. Odilo wanted to know if the game reserve had what rangers called the Big Five: lion, leopard, rhino, elephant and buffalo.

'It does,' Martine said proudly. 'We don't have any cheetahs though. We do have three leopards – a mother and two cubs. They were given to Sawubona by a wildlife park that went out of business. I've seen the cubs but never the mother. She's very elusive.'

'Here in the Matopos, we have the Small Five,' Ngwenya told her with a grin.

'The *Small* Five?'

He counted them off on his fingers. 'The Leopard Tortoise, the Rhino Beetle, the Ant Lion, the Elephant Shrew and the Buffalo Weaver!'

Everyone laughed and for a moment the gloom over the village was lifted.

Before Ngwenya could continue, the dogs bounded up barking. Martine glanced nervously at Ben.

'Who's there?' Odilo called out.

Out of the night strode a tall young man dressed very smartly in a shirt, tie and trilby. He had a handsome face, blighted by a perpetual sneer, and smelled quite strongly of cologne.

Martine stared at him in shock. It was Ngwenya's cousin.

The cousin who wanted the leopard dead.

'Good evening, good evening,' he said pleasantly, though it was obvious that no one in the circle was pleased to see him. 'I am in time for supper? That is great news. Thank you, Mercy. It's very nice of you to make it for me.'

He unfolded a plastic sheet from his pocket, sat cross-legged on it and took off his hat. 'Pass me a bowl, Ngwenya.'

Ngwenya made no move to hand it to him, but he took one anyway and helped himself to a large portion of everything. He was sucking the marrow out of a chicken bone when his dark eyes alighted on the young strangers.

He flashed Martine and Ben a sinister smile. Thrusting out his hand so they had no choice but to take it, he said. 'My name is Griffin. How do you do?'

'What are you doing here, Griffin?' Ngwenya demanded. 'You are not welcome.'

Griffin did not seem in the least offended by this comment. He bit the top off another chicken drumstick, drained it of marrow and said placidly, 'Ah, my cousin, you will be singing a different song when I come home with Lobengula's treasure. I will be welcome then, I am sure. Any day now I will be returning with sacks full of diamonds and gold sovereigns and then all of you will want to be my friend.'

'Griffin, my son, you are talking nonsense,' Odilo said in his quiet way, and Martine started at the revelation that shy, mournful Odilo was father to this sharp-dressing vagabond.

Mercy's face was expressionless. She heaved herself to her feet and went to her hut to be with her child. Odilo soon followed.

The atmosphere around the fire was strained. For a while there was no sound but the crackling of the smouldering wood. Then, to Martine's astonishment, Ben asked, 'What will you do with the treasure if you find it, Griffin?'

Griffin seemed pleased to be asked. He said grandly, 'I will buy a Mercedes Benz and a house with many bathrooms and a flat-screen television in Bulawayo. I will fly to England first class and buy some suits for myself. Some cigarettes. Some whisky.'

Ngwenya said abruptly, 'Lobengula's treasure belongs to the tribe; to the Ndebele people. If you find it, you will have to give it to the chiefs. The elders will come together and will have to make a decision whether or not to keep it.'

Griffin gave a scathing laugh. 'Are you mad, Ngwenya? Do you think that if I find gold and diamonds I will share it with those doddering old men? They know nothing. Chief Nyoni will probably put it back in the ground. Or maybe he will use it to buy false teeth. No, if I find the treasure I will keep it for me and my friends. If you want to share it, you must look for it yourself.'

'I don't want to find the treasure,' Ngwenya told him. 'All over Africa, men have gone crazy with greed trying to follow this false promise. We do not want this to happen in our tribe. If the treasure is never found, it may be for the best.'

The conversation was getting heated and Martine was afraid that a fight would break out, but it was interrupted by a swirl of black, white and yellow. Before Martine could register what was happening, the hornbill had swooped out of the night and landed on her knee, using the creases in her jeans as brakes.

'Magnus!' she cried, inexplicably cheered by the reappearance of the odd, serious bird, her last connection with her grandmother and Sadie. 'How did you find us?'

'We think his nest is in the place we call Rock Rabbit Hill in our language,' said Ngwenya. 'It is very close to here so perhaps he spotted you when he was on his way home to roost for the evening. Rock Rabbit Hill is riddled with holes and tunnels. If you fall into one, you might never come out. Some guests at the retreat who have lost their jewellery have tried to locate this nest, but it is very unsafe to climb up this hill and no one has ever managed. I myself think that when the nest is found it will be full of bottle tops and other rubbish.'

Martine rubbed the top of the hornbill's head and his eyelashes fluttered up and down in ecstasy.

Griffin wiped chicken grease from his mouth and scrutinized her as if she were a specimen under a microscope. 'I have just come from visiting the witchdoctor, who will be coming here shortly. He told me that there were some children staying in my uncle's village tonight, and that he has been hearing some stories that one of these children, a white girl, rides a giraffe back home in South Africa. He threw the bones and they helped him to remember the Zulu legend about the child who rides the white giraffe having power over all the animals.'

He nodded at Magnus. 'You are obviously a friend to the wild birds. Does this mean you are the girl in the ancestor's story? Is your giraffe in South Africa white?'

Martine didn't respond. She didn't want him, of all people, knowing anything about her or Jemmy. She hoped that if she ignored him he'd get the message and leave her alone, but Ngwenya innocently put her on the spot.

'A *white* giraffe?' he exclaimed. 'An albino one? Is this true, Martine? *Now* I understand. Now it becomes clear. When Gogo said you rode a giraffe, I wasn't too sure whether to believe her. Then I saw how the horses loved you and what a good rider you are, and I thought that maybe some people had helped you to train a giraffe from when it was very young. Nobody told me it was a white one. Is this correct? Are you the child in the Zulu legend?'

Forced to respond, Martine said: 'Trust me, I don't have power over any animals. Sometimes I help them a little, that's all.'

'Which way do you help them?' Griffin wanted to know.

Martine had no intention of answering him. 'Would you like me to wash the dishes?' she asked Mercy's sister.

'Maybe we can help each other, Martine,' Griffin persisted. 'There is an animal I would like to have power over. If you assist me, maybe I can let you have a little piece of treasure. A gold sovereign, perhaps, or a diamond.'

That was the final straw for Ngwenya. He knew full well that the animal his cousin wanted power over was Khan. 'That is enough, Griffin,' he shouted. 'I told you that you are not welcome here and now it is time for you to leave.'

Martine expected Griffin to protest, but he jumped up in one lithe, easy movement, took off his hat and bowed. 'Goodbye, friends,' he said. 'Next time you see me I shall be a rich man.'

Turning on his heel, he flashed another sinister smile. Martine had a bad feeling it was intended for her.

Not surprisingly, she and Ben found it nearly impossible to sleep. They were still awake, discussing the events of the day and how best to tackle the problem of getting into the Lazy J, an hour after saying goodnight to Ngwenya. The horse wrangler had gone to check on the retreat, some twenty minutes' ride away. He was planning to spend the night there and return at the crack of dawn. Martine had been afraid he'd try to stop them; that he'd tell them they were insane to imagine they could sneak into the hunter's ranch and attempt to find evidence that the Rat was blackmailing Sadie and behind the arrests at Black Eagle. But all he said was, 'Martine and Ben, I think you are both *penga*. This is the word we have in Zimbabwe for people who are mad. But if you are *penga*, then so am I. We will leave before sunrise.'

Martine and Ben were making another attempt to close their eyes when they heard a commotion outside.

Ben bounded up and pushed back the hessian cloth that covered the doorway. 'Martine, there are a lot of people milling around the fire and waving their hands in the air as if they're angry or upset. Either the police are on their way or baby Emelia is really ill. I think we should see what's going on.'

They put on their sweatshirts and went out into the cold night air. As they neared the fire, they saw the witchdoctor. He had his back to them and was sitting opposite Mercy and Odilo, whose faces were tense with anxiety. The villagers were gathered in a circle behind them, buzzing with anticipation. Baby Emelia lay between Mercy and Odilo, wrapped in a sheepskin rug.

Nobody noticed Ben and Martine approaching through the darkness – nobody, that is, except the witchdoctor. After holding up his hand for silence, he slowly and very deliberately turned to face the young outsiders. There was something very ancient and tribal about his necklace of horns, belt of ostrich feathers and leopard-skin kilt. It was as if the modern world had never touched him. It was impossible to say how old he was. He could have been ninety or thirty.

Martine found herself looking at his leopard-skin kilt and thinking about something Ngwenya had told her. He'd explained that the kilts were handed down from one generation to the next. The hide of leopards was specially chosen because the leopard was regarded by the Ndebele as the politest and most respectful of all the animals, and the witchdoctors wished to show the same politeness and respect to the ancestral spirits. Martine's own opinion was that it might have been more polite and respectful not to rob the leopard of its skin, but she'd known better than to say that.

The witchdoctor fixed her with a fierce glare, as if he'd known her in a past life and she'd done him a great wrong. 'There is no work for you here,' he said.

The villagers murmured in alarm, and one or two motioned her and Ben away. The witchdoctor held up his hand for silence again. He turned his back on Martine, took a swig from a brown bottle at his side, removed his ceremonial pouch, scattered some bones on the ground and began to chant.

Martine and Ben retreated to the shadows, feeling like unwanted guests intruding on a sacred ritual. Which, in effect, they were. But after half an hour of chanting they were so cold they dared to creep back to the fireside.

Nobody chased them away. They were too absorbed in another spectacle. In between chants, the witchdoctor had continued to take long swallows from his brown bottle, and two other empty bottles of what Ben suspected was 'some powerful homebrewed moonshine' lay on the earth beside him. His eyes were red and streaming. He was swaying over his bones and his chanting sounded slurred.

'It's her ssshhtumach,' he mumbled at last. 'Sh-sh-she has shtumach flu. She needs—' and he reeled off a plant name Martine recognized. His glazed eyes singled out Martine in the crowd. He lifted a forefinger and waggled it at her, as if to say, 'I'm warning you.' Then he keeled over and began snoring loudly.

Mercy recovered first. 'That drunken idiot!' she shouted. 'My baby is dying and he can't control his thirst for this poison for even one night.'

She aimed several kicks at the sprawling figure before a couple of villagers restrained her. Tears began to stream down her face. Odilo put his arms around her and looked as though he might weep too. In the sheepskin rug, the baby whimpered feebly.

'I might be able to help,' Martine offered in a small voice.

She spoke so softly that nobody heard her above the babble of voices. Martine was too shy to repeat what she'd said, but Ben went over to the sad couple. 'Mercy and Odilo, Martine might be able to help,' he told them.

This time Odilo and some of the villagers turned, although most seemed displeased at the interruption.

'You have a power with babies?' Odilo asked doubtfully.

Martine shook her head. 'No, I don't. But in my survival kit I have medicine made from the plant the witchdoctor mentioned. My friend Grace, a South African *sangoma*, gave it to me.'

Odilo was unsure, but between sobs Mercy urged her to fetch it quickly. Martine raced to get it from the hut and unzipped it in the firelight. There were gasps as she removed her pink Maglite, Swiss Army knife, silver whistle, compass, magnifying glass, tube of superglue, and three small brown bottles: one for headaches and pain, one to treat Bilharzia, a disease found in Zimbabwean rivers, and one for stomach ailments.

Mercy read the label on the stomach one, removed the cork from the top of it and sniffed. Evidently it met with her approval.

'Odilo and I will take Emelia to our hut and talk about whether we should take a chance and give it to her,' she told Martine. 'It must be our decision.'

Martine sank down beside Ben to wait, warming her hands on the fire. One of the villagers handed her a mug of tea and its fragrant sweetness temporarily revived her. But not for long. She checked her watch and realized that she and Ben had been up for twenty hours. So many things had happened. It felt like the longest day on earth. It was hard to believe that nineteen hours ago she'd come face to face with the largest leopard ever recorded.

By the time Odilo returned, she could no longer see straight she was so tired, and Ben was so sleepy he was nodding like one of those nodding dogs in cars.

'Mercy says to thank you very much,' Odilo told Martine. But her heart sank when he added ominously, 'Whatever happens . . .'

She opened her mouth to say that she wasn't a doctor or even a *sangoma* and maybe it had been a bad idea to hand over Grace's stomach *muti* without a medical practitioner's diagnosis, but Odilo guessed what was troubling her and said, 'Go to sleep. Have faith in your *sangoma* friend's medicine. There is nothing more we can do. We must wait for the *muti* to do its work.'

As the moon crept higher in a sky that was more white than blue-black it had so many stars in it, the whole village slumbered. The only creature still awake was Magnus. Frustrated that Martine had disappeared into a hut and seemed not to be coming out again, the hornbill was strolling about in search of entertainment. He found nothing to interest him until he reached the cooking area, where the contents of Martine's survival pouch still winked in the dying embers of the fire.

Unnoticed, the hornbill hopped nearer.

Martine tossed and turned for the remainder of the night on the hard, unfamiliar bed, agonizing over her grandmother and whether or not she'd done the right thing giving Grace's *muti* to the sick baby. She fell asleep just before dawn and was woken minutes later by Ben. 'Emelia is much better and is drinking her breakfast,' he said. 'Ngwenya is back and has heard the whole story. He says that Odilo is smiling from one ear to the other for the first time since he lost his job.'

As glad as Martine was to receive this news, it was agony to be wrenched from her dreams after a mere catnap. She was as keen as anyone to get to the Lazy J and search for answers, but she longed for some proper sleep. The epic drive to Zimbabwe, the strain of keeping her encounter with Khan secret, Gwyn Thomas's arrest and the witchdoctor's frightening reaction to her, had all been too much.

She could just imagine what the conversations would be like when she and Ben returned to Caracal Junior. Luke and Lucy would be going on about surfing and sunbathing in the Mediterranean, Jake would be talking non-stop about rugby camp, and Claudius would be full of tall tales about hiking in the Drakensberg Mountains with his dad.

Finally they'd get round to asking what she and Ben had done on their vacation and Martine would pipe up: 'Well, let me see. First, Ben was nearly smashed to bits falling down a waterfall, then we saw a lion being shot in cold blood, and next day I was nearly mauled by a leopard. Oh, and my grandmother was taken away to jail by two corrupt policemen, and Ben and I had to hide in a remote village, and while we were there a baby developed a raging fever and I had to help save it. Apart from that, we had a very relaxing time.'

Ngwenya interrupted her thoughts by putting a mug of tea and a bowl of *mielie*-meal porridge in front of her.

'Eat quickly,' he said. 'We must go to the Lazy J before the sun gets up.'

Ben joined her. He'd endured a 'bird bath' using a bucket of ice-cold water, and he was shivering in the crisp morning air. 'How are you feeling?' he asked, rubbing the goosebumps on his arms. 'You got even less sleep than I did.'

'I'm scared,' Martine admitted. 'I'm scared for us but mainly I'm frightened for Khan, my grandmother, and Sadie. What if we can't help them? We're up against corrupt policemen, blackmailing hunters and all this wilderness. There seems to be a different set of rules in Zimbabwe. The law doesn't seem to mean anything here.'

She swallowed a few spoonfuls of porridge. 'How 'bout you? How do you feel about today?'

'I don't think Rex Ratcliffe should be allowed to get away with making so many people and animals suffer,' Ben said. 'Somebody has to try to stop him and it may as well be us. I know it seems impossible, but I think we're a pretty good team when it comes to doing the impossible. Let's visualize the outcome we want and try to make it happen. We want your grandmother and Sadie to come home safely. That's No.1. But we also want to save Khan and find him a place where he can live in freedom, away from any hunters. Try it, Martine. Try to picture it.'

Martine closed her eyes and conjured up an image of Sawubona. She visualized herself and the white giraffe standing beside Gwyn Thomas watching the sun come up over the lake. Jemmy was resting his head on her shoulder. Her grandmother was pointing at the hippos and saying something that made Martine laugh.

Next she tried to picture Khan in a place of safety. In Martine's opinion, Sawubona was the best game sanctuary in the world, so that's where she saw him. He was lying on a boulder high up on the mountain that overlooked the lake, his forelegs stretched out like a Sphinx, watching her, Gwyn Thomas and the white giraffe. In Martine's vision, he got up and began to make his way down the slope, dislodging a rock as he did so.

Then the picture went fuzzy. Martine squinted at the image in her head, trying to conjure it up again, but it was gone.

She went back to the hut to collect her survival kit and only remembered when she got there that she'd left it by the fireside the previous night. She was on her way out again when she noticed a baby tortoise heading towards her. Martine gave a cry of delight. 'You're so sweet,' she said. 'Where did you come from?'

She picked it up and saw the tortoise had something strapped to its back. It was too dark inside the hut to see it, so she carried it over to the light. Ngwenya had hung a lantern from a hook on the wall. She lifted the tortoise to the flickering glow and had to bite back a scream. Strapped to its back was a perfectly crafted miniature coffin.

Ben came up, carrying her survival kit. He stared at the tortoise in bewilderment. 'Is this someone's idea of a sick joke? Where did you find it?'

'Someone put it in our hut,' Martine said, shivering. She was so sickened she wanted to hurl the tortoise into the bushes, but she knew very well it wasn't the tortoise's fault. She untied the coffin, crushed it under her boot, and set the tortoise carefully on its way. 'It's a warning.

No prizes for guessing who sent it.'

'The witchdoctor?'

'The witchdoctor. By giving the *muti* to Mercy and Odilo, he probably feels I've humiliated him.'

'He humiliated himself,' Ben reminded her. 'It's not your fault he was drunk.'

'All the same, we need to be on our guard.'

She blew out the lamp and fastened her survival kit around her waist. Through the half dark came the clip-clop of horses' hooves. Sirocco's leather reins were thrust into her hands.

'Come,' said Ngwenya. 'We must hurry.'

They reached the Lazy J at six a.m., tethering the horses and walking the last kilometre. It was already light and Ben was concerned that they were too late to do any meaningful searching, but Ngwenya had timed it so they arrived while the hunters were out shooting. He estimated that they had about an hour until the men came back, laden with the bloody carcasses of wildlife they'd killed, for a meaty fry-up of crocodile steak and buffalo sausage.

'We must split up in case we are discovered,' he said. 'It is easier for two to rescue one than for one to rescue two.'

Martine was about to object, but Ben got in before her.

'Sorry, Ngwenya,' he said. 'I made that mistake at the

leopard cave and I'm not going to do it again. Martine and I can't be separated. What we're about to attempt is very risky. If we can't do it together, we can't do it at all.'

'I agree,' Martine said. 'I'm not going anywhere without Ben.'

Ngwenya was amused by their protectiveness towards one another. 'As you wish. I will go to the lodge where the tourists stay and try to get into the office, where there might be some records.'

'Great,' Martine said. 'We'll go and check out the animal enclosure.'

Ngwenya bridled. 'You will stay away from the lions and cheetahs? It is bad enough that you have persuaded me to bring you here. Please do not get into any trouble with the animals. Just because Magnus and the horses like you, it does not mean lions and cheetahs will be your friends.'

Martine smiled angelically. 'Don't worry, Ngwenya. We'll look but we won't touch.'

Getting into the Lazy J was simplicity itself. The guard at the gatehouse was accustomed to people arriving by vehicle, not on foot. He never even lifted his eyes from his newspaper as they sneaked under the barrier and sprinted across the parking area that lay between the razor-wire-topped perimeter fence and the gates of the hunting lodge.

Ngwenya turned to Martine. 'I hope that your grandmother and Gogo are not angry with me for bringing you here.'

'They won't be,' she told him. 'Especially if we can find

evidence showing that Mr Ratcliffe is trying to drive Sadie out of business and sell Khan's skin for thousands of US dollars.'

'Be very careful,' Ngwenya said. 'The Rat is a wicked man. You've seen what he is capable of. If he catches you, I don't know what he might do.'

Crouching low, he followed the wall around to the tourist lodge. Ben and Martine wasted no time. They slipped beneath the turnstile into the wildlife enclosure. Their plan was to stay out of sight if possible, but act casually if they were caught and brazen it out.

As soon as they entered the concrete and steel enclosure, they realized they were in a hunting zoo. The majority of the cages were filled with lions and cheetahs, but there were also three black rhino in a paddock, and a walled-off pond where half a dozen crocodiles could be seen basking in the sun.

The male lions charged at the wire mesh of their cages, snarling with rage. The cheetahs paced up and down their runs relentlessly, as though their prison had driven them demented.

The animals were well kept and their cages clean, but their eyes were frantic with fear. Martine couldn't stop thinking about the shot lion, his life leaking out onto the hunter's boot while the big-bellied man posed for photographs. She knew that the other animals knew what was going to happen to them. Day after day, they heard the dying roars of their companions and had to wait, trembling, for the clink of keys that would mean they too were being summoned before the executioner.

'Martine,' Ben said. 'Someone's coming.'

They flew down the corridor between the runs, and up the steps of a storage room beside the crocodile pond, darting inside in the nick of time. A man carrying a bucket pushed his way through the turnstile and made his way along the rows of animals, whistling as he sloshed water into their drinking containers. When his bucket was empty he went out the way he came in.

As soon as he was gone, they began their search in earnest. Like everything else at the Lazy J, the storage room was clean and tidy. Half of it was a basic office. There was a desk and chair, a filing cabinet, and a couple of boxes overflowing with glossy brochures describing the Lazy J as the 'ultimate safari experience'. The other half was piled high with sacks of a well-known brand of dog food.

'It's a cheap way of feeding lions and cheetahs,' Martine explained to Ben. 'Lots of wildlife parks do it, but it isn't the best thing for the animals.'

But it was the electrical panel on the back wall that interested them most. It featured two rows of red lights numbered up to thirty. One row was labelled: 'Gate Open'. The other read: 'Gate Shut'.

Ben looked at Martine. 'Are you thinking what I'm thinking?'

Martine gave a nervous laugh. 'It's very tempting, but we can't set the lions free . . . Can we?'

Ben went over to the desk and sat in the chair. 'It's a nice idea. Unfortunately they might end up eating Rex Ratcliffe or one of his hunters and that wouldn't be a good thing.'

'Even though they deserve it,' said Martine.

'Even though they deserve it.'

Ben opened the journal on the desk and started flicking through it. 'This is sickening. It seems to be a record of daily hunts and kills. On a single day last week, they shot five kudu, one lion, two sable antelope and two elephants.'

'Is there any mention of Khan?'

Ben flicked through once again. 'Not that I can see.'

'Try checking the dates still to come. Maybe it's scheduled,' said Martine, taking a quick peek out of the door. She saw no one apart from the keeper who was pouring water into the rhinos' trough.

Ben finished his search. 'No, nothing . . . Hold on a minute. The entry for tomorrow is different to all the rest. It's written in capital letters and it says: OPERATION WILDCAT – 5 a.m. Elephant Rock.'

'Elephant Rock!' cried Martine. 'That's on Black Eagle land. How dare they trespass on Sadie's property. That proves that Rex Ratcliffe had her and my grandmother arrested to get them out of the way. And Operation Wild Cat has to mean they're going after Khan.'

Ben tore the page out of the journal and put it in his pocket. 'I'm taking this as evidence. It has the Lazy J logo at the top and it might hold up in court.'

Footsteps rang on the concrete path outside. Ben barely had time to dart around the desk and pretend to be studying a poster of an elephant before a man with a bushy blond moustache strode in.

He seemed stunned to see them – so stunned that it

took him a second or two to react. Then he growled, 'Who are you and what do you think you're doing in here?'

'Good morning, sir,' Ben said smoothly. 'I apologize if we're not supposed to be in here. Our parents are up at the lodge and we were curious to see how a real hunting operation worked.'

'Were you now,' the man said sarcastically. 'I suppose that's okay then. And how might I assist you?'

'We were just wondering if you had a brochure,' Ben said.

'A brochure? Yes, of course you can have a brochure.' He handed Ben one from the box. 'What did you say your parents' names were?'

'Jones,' Martine said. 'Mr and Mrs Jones.'

'My parents' names are Moyo,' added Ben. 'Mr and Mrs Moyo.'

'Moyo and Jones?' he repeated slowly, as if he was trying to place their faces. 'That's very interesting. The reason it's so interesting is because I happen to be the duty manager and I can categorically confirm that nobody by either of those names is staying at the lodge.'

'We're not staying,' Martine explained. 'We've just popped in for meal and a safari.'

He chuckled. 'Good try, but we have a no-children policy here and it's very strictly enforced. Kids tend to get a bit weepy over all the dead animals.'

He picked up the telephone. 'Security? Yes, we have two intruders in the lion and cheetah compound.'

Martine glanced at Ben and moved her chin

fractionally towards the electrical board.

'I think that's a very good idea,' Ben said out loud.

The man put down the receiver. 'You think what is a very good idea? Calling security?'

He never got to finish his sentence. Before he could move a muscle, Ben had flown like quicksilver around the desk, hit the row of switches labelled 'Gate Open', and was out of the door with Martine behind him.

Ben had a split second to say, 'Martine, let him come after me, then lock the door so he can't get back in to lock the cages. Climb over the wall – I'll meet you on the other side.'

Martine almost collided with the duty manager as he clattered down the steps, but he made only a half-hearted attempt to grab her before racing after Ben, the real object of his wrath. As Ben neared the first of the cages, two security guards appeared at the turnstile. The manager gestured for them to catch Ben. It had belatedly struck him that his own priority should be preventing the lions and cheetahs from escaping. He tore back to the storeroom, but it was too late. Martine had locked the door and was sitting on top of the wall with the key.

'Give that to me,' shouted the manager, dancing with fury below her. 'Have you any idea what you've done?'

'You want it?' Martine said, holding the key out of his reach. 'Go and get it.'

She threw it into the crocodile pen where, by a complete fluke, it hit a rock and ricocheted into the open mouth of a basking reptile. His jaws snapped shut and he gulped. Martine took advantage of the manager's apoplexy to jump down the other side of the wall and make a run for the car park.

Her biggest fear was that she wouldn't be able to find Ben, but he came flying over the turnstile like a hurdler and was just as relieved to see her.

'Where are the guards?' Martine asked in panic.

Ben grinned. 'I believe they were detained by one or two lions.'

A moving cloud of dust on the horizon wiped the smile off his face. 'The hunters,' he said. 'They're on their way back.'

He took Martine's hand and they ran down the driveway and past the guardhouse. This time the guard did see them, but his attention was diverted when two cheetahs streaked by, followed by a lumbering rhino. The cheetahs slipped under the barrier; the rhino crashed straight through it. They were so preoccupied with the sight of the open savannah and a chance at freedom that they ignored Martine and Ben. As Martine and Ben headed after them, they could hear the guard yelling into his radio for back-up.

Ben was a champion long distance runner and he sprinted easily along the road towards the thick bush that would give them cover. Martine, on the other hand, was one of Caracal Junior's slowest athletes. Halfway back to the horses, her legs started to feel like lead and she developed a stitch. A couple of camouflage-painted four-wheel drives zoomed into view. They were coming from the opposite direction.

Martine paused, trying to catch her breath. 'You go on

without me,' she said to Ben. 'Find Ngwenya and get word to Sadie and Gwyn Thomas about the hunt at Black Eagle tomorrow. I'll be fine. Even Rex Ratcliffe must draw the line at putting children in jail.'

'Don't be crazy,' said Ben. 'There's absolutely no way I'm leaving you. Remember what Grace told you.'

They started to run again, but there were shouts from behind and one of the safari vehicles left the road and roared after them through the bush. Martine's stitch became unbearable and she pulled up, gasping.

'I can't go on,' she panted as they entered a grove of trees. 'Please, Ben, I'm begging you, save yourself. For Khan's sake.'

'No,' said Ben, gripping her hand more tightly. 'We'll face them together.'

The safari vehicle ploughed through the long yellow grass and screeched to a halt beneath an old mopani tree. Five men in khaki clothes spilled off the back and surrounded them. None of the men spoke. They just stared at the vehicle expectantly.

The passenger door opened slowly and out came a pair of alligator-skin cowboy boots, followed by their owner: a gaunt figure with unnaturally white skin, sporting a safari suit and slicked-down black hair. He had the weirdest face Martine had ever seen. Every feature was sharp and thrust forward so that they came together in a point, at the tip of which was a bloodless mouth and two yellow buck teeth. He was like the product of a rodent-human genetic experiment that had gone horribly wrong.

Leaning on a cane, he walked stiffly over to Ben and Martine and glared down at them from a great height. 'Are these them?' he enquired, his voice high-pitched with outrage. 'Are these the children who have jeopardized my entire hunting operation?'

'Mr Rat, I presume,' Martine said.

15

'Rat*cliffe*,' squeaked the rodent man. 'The name is Rat*cliffe*.'

That was as far as he got because from above their heads came a roar so terrifying that Mr Rat's cane dropped from his fingers and one of the guides fainted on the spot.

Then Khan dropped from the sky.

Martine caught a rapid-fire glimpse of unforgettable images, the most striking of which was the golden body of the leopard completely covering Mr Rat, as if the hunter had suddenly acquired the leopard-skin coat he was after. Then she and Ben were running for their lives.

They swerved through the trees, along a narrow path and up to the rear gate of Black Eagle, where the horses were waiting.

'Where is Ngwenya?' Martine fretted.

'I am here,' the horse wrangler replied, running up behind them with a large plastic canister in his hand. He, too, was breathing hard.

He put his hands on their shoulders and started laughing. 'I saw everything,' he said. 'I was waiting in the trees for you and I watched the jeep chase after you. I heard Mr Ratcliffe and his guides threatening you. I was waiting for my chance to do something when I noticed the leopard sitting in the mopani tree. I saw him getting ready to strike. Oh, Martine, he is the most beautiful animal I have ever seen. His colours! His coat glows like it is on fire and his spots are like black diamonds.'

Martine was too upset to be interested in the merits of Khan's coat. 'Did you see what happened to him?' she said. 'I'm petrified they might try to shoot him.'

Ngwenya grinned. 'Don't worry, my friend, there was no shooting. One of the guides went to get his rifle and Khan opened up his chest with a swipe of his paw. That man will be spending many months in hospital, I think. The others carried him and Mr Ratcliffe back to the car. Mr Ratcliffe was bleeding and whimpering like a puppy, but I was close enough to hear him say, "Operation Wildcat must go ahead as planned." I don't know what that means.'

'We do,' Ben said, handing Ngwenya the page from the journal. 'The hunt for Khan starts at five tomorrow morning. Somehow we have to stop it.'

Ngwenya scanned the entry. 'Elephant Rock? They are meeting at Elephant Rock? Who are they to trespass on Gogo's land?'

'That's what we said,' Martine told him. 'The good thing about it is it proves that the Rat had Sadie and my grandmother arrested to get them out of the way. All we need to do now is get the information to the authorities.'

Ngwenya held up his plastic container. It sloshed with brown liquid. 'That's what this is for. I found two things at the Lazy J. I found an Ndebele waiter who had some very interesting things to say about the poison he was paid to put in a water tank for cattle at Black Eagle. He admits he put a little in the tank but felt too guilty to add the rest. His father and his father before him were cattlemen, and he felt that by hurting cows he was dishonouring his ancestors' memory.

'He hid the bottle in a baobab tree on Black Eagle land. He promises to show the police where it is if I can guarantee to find him another job.'

'You said you found two things,' Ben said. 'Is the other one petrol?'

'It is. I am going to ride to the retreat at Black Eagle, fill up one of the vehicles, and go to Bulawayo to give this information to the District Attorney. I have heard he is an honest man. With any luck, your grandmother and Gogo will be home by this evening.'

'We'll come with you,' Martine said.

Ngwenya shook his head. 'In case there is trouble with the police, it is better for you to stay with Mercy and

Odilo. Before I go to Bulawayo, I will accompany you to the village.'

'We'll be fine on our own,' Martine said. 'I think you should go to Bulawayo right away. The sooner you can persuade the DA to release my grandmother and Sadie, the better.'

Ngwenya wasn't convinced. 'You will be safe by yourselves?'

Ben smiled at him. 'Safe as houses.'

After Ngwenya had galloped away on Red Mist, they began the long trek to the village through the rocks and hills of Black Eagle. Martine would have liked to gallop as fast as the terrain allowed, but Ben's riding was not up to that yet and Mambo refused to cooperate.

'We should have brought Cassidy,' Martine grumbled as Mambo plodded tiredly along, giving an Oscar-worthy performance of a poor, abused pony who'd only ever known hardship and toil, when the truth was that he was fat, spoilt and spent the greater portion of his time eating and sleeping.

'It's not the horse, it's me,' Ben said charitably. 'I don't think I'm cut out to be a rider. Next time I'm bringing a bicycle.'

'You're too nice,' Martine told him. 'They know they can get away with murder with you, that's the problem.'

'You're an angel to them and it works for you,' Ben

pointed out. 'I think the difference is that you can communicate with them. They understand you. Even the leopard understands you. That's why he came to your rescue.'

'He wasn't rescuing me,' protested Martine. 'He doesn't even know me. He probably spotted Mr Rat and thought he was looking at the largest rodent he'd ever seen and fancied a meal.'

Ben regarded her intently. 'Are you sure? I mean, are you sure that Khan doesn't know you?'

'I'm sorry,' said Martine, ashamed that she'd hidden it from her best friend. 'I was waiting for the right time to tell you. Ben, he could have killed me, but he didn't. He stood over me and I felt as though I looked into his soul. It was so magical and frightening I didn't know how to put it into words.'

Ben smiled at her. 'You didn't have to. I understood.'

'Ben?'

'Yes.'

'We have to save him.'

'We will. I promise.'

'Ben?'

He laughed. 'Yes, Martine.'

'Thank you for staying with me when the hunters came after us. You could easily have got away. You're a fantastic runner.'

'You would have done the same for me.'

She smiled at him, 'Yes, I would.'

A strange expression crossed Ben's face. 'Martine?'

There was something in his voice that made her

halt Sirocco. 'Ben, what is it? You look as if you've remembered something scary.'

'It was Khan I saw that day, wasn't it?' he said. 'The day I fell down the waterfall, I mean. The drawing on the rocks was Sadie's leopard, I just know it was. But who could have put it there – behind the curtain of water? I was nearly killed simply leaning over the edge to look at it. Do you think it was some kind of prediction? Do you think Grace was right and our destinies are connected in some way?'

'I'm not sure,' Martine answered, although she actually was sure. She was quite certain she and Ben were connected, and that he saw the sketch when he was meant to see it; that he saw it for a reason. As to who put it there, well, it could have been done a century before by the same people who'd predicted Khan would pounce on her.

Before she could say any more to Ben, Sirocco shied violently. If riding Jemmy hadn't taught Martine to have lightning reaction times she would have had a nasty fall. As it was she ended up with her legs on either side of Sirocco's ears and had to climb off the mare and remount.

The grass rustled and Ngwenya's cousin and his *shamwaris* stepped onto the path. Griffin was still dressed like a gangster, in a trilby and waistcoat, although all were very grimy.

'So it's true then?' he said. 'The child who rides the white giraffe does have power over all the animals. Horses, birds, even leopards.' He laughed. 'News travels quickly on the bush telegraph.'

'What do you want?' Ben demanded, moving Mambo as close to Sirocco as he could.

Griffin reached up and grabbed the bridles of both horses, and Martine caught a whiff of cologne. 'I want your friend to help me with a little problem I have.'

Martine was livid. She knew that the tiniest pressure of her heel would send the Arab mare hurtling into the hills, leaving Griffin and his greedy, treasure-seeking buddies spitting dirt, but that would mean abandoning Ben and Mambo to their mercy and never in a million years would she do that.

'I know what you want,' she said scornfully. 'You want to use me to control the leopard so that you can find him and kill him. You think that Khan will lead you to Lobengula's treasure.'

Griffin smiled his wolfish smile. 'So you've heard about our plans. Maybe you are correct; maybe you are not. I told you that if you assist us with the leopard, we might give you some gold or maybe a diamond.'

'I wouldn't assist you if my life depended on it.'

'It might,' he said matter-of-factly.

16

An hour after Operation Wildcat had officially started, Martine was balanced on a crate in a boarded up storeroom of what had once been a shop, peering through a vent at their captors. Two of them were asleep on the old shop counter, one wrapped in a tatty blanket, the other on an old mattress. Griffin had not been up long himself. He was out on the veranda, poking half-heartedly at the ashes of the previous night's fire and clutching at his head as if he was trying to make sure it belonged to him.

Martine hoped that he had an extremely painful hangover or, better still, a migraine requiring a lobotomy. She was furious with him. She and Ben had been held captive by him and his fiendish friends for almost twenty-four hours, and every one of those hours had been misery. They'd been kidnapped at about nine o'clock in the morning and denied food or water until six in the evening because Martine refused to give Griffin any information on her gift.

'It is up to you if you want to starve yourself and your friend,' he said. 'It is easy for you to talk.'

'We are not criminals,' one of his friends told her. 'Don't worry, we are not going to hurt you. We are only looking for treasure that is lying in the ground, wasted, when it is the right of any Ndebele man with initiative to enjoy its beautiful golden fruit if he locates it.'

In the end, she and Ben were so thirsty and hungry that Martine made up a story about how she had the power to read tea leaves if they were brewed with aloe juice and lucky beans. She explained that the liquid was very poisonous and could not be drunk, but that she would strain it away using a special method. Griffin immediately rushed off to gather all three items, and Martine pored over the mug and pretended to be shocked to read in the leaves that Mr Ratcliffe was organizing a big hunt for the leopard which would leave Elephant Rock at five a.m. next morning.

This information earned her and Ben as much water as they could drink and a dinner of sadza and tripe and other cow innards, which they couldn't eat. The meat was so revolting that the smell alone made them nauseous, although they did force down a little sadza.

Martine had told Griffin about the hunt for a reason. She'd gambled that he would want to get to the leopard before Ratcliffe's men did, and that she and Ben might still have a chance to escape and save Khan. It didn't occur to her that the treasure seekers would be so eager to get to Khan first that she and Ben would be dragged up and down every hill in the Matopos until one o'clock in the morning in a bid to unearth him. By that time, Martine, who felt as if she hadn't slept in weeks, was nearly sobbing with tiredness.

Since then, she and Ben had been locked in the dusty, windowless storeroom with nothing but a bottle of water, a wooden crate and a couple of sacks. The sacks were Griffin's idea of bedding. Outside in the ruined store, the treasure seekers had drunk Zambezi beer until the small hours.

Martine had not slept a wink. One of the many things that had kept her awake was the frustrating fact that her survival kit was still tied to Sirocco's saddle. She'd taken to hanging it there when she was riding, reasoning that she could impale herself on her Swiss Army knife if she fell off and landed on it. She hadn't counted on Griffin and Co showing up.

Now she was a wreck. Her hair was standing on end and she would have given anything for a shower. Squinting through the vent, she was pleased to see that Griffin looked even worse. Ben, on the other hand, was sitting cross-legged on the floor with his palms on his thighs and his eyes closed. He was the picture of tranquillity.

'I don't understand how you can sit there so peacefully when the Rat's hunters are out searching for Khan,' Martine said accusingly, climbing down from her unsteady perch. 'He might be lying bleeding somewhere. Don't you care what happens to him?'

Ben opened his eyes. 'I think you already know the answer to that.'

He sprang gracefully to his feet and started to inspect every inch of their windowless cell – walls, floor and ceiling.

'Now what are you doing?'

Ben didn't reply. He put his nose close to a rusty water pipe and stared at it so hard, for so long, he went cross-eyed.

Martine became concerned that the stresses of the last week had taken more of a toll on him than she'd realized. 'Ben, come and sit down,' she said. 'I'm sorry about that comment about Khan. I know you care about him as much as I do.'

Ben continued to stare into the pipe. 'Martine, what did Ngwenya tell us about the Enemy of Lions?'

'What are you talking about?'

'I'm serious. Can you remember what he said?'

She sighed. 'Sure. He said, "Where you find these ants, you won't find any lions. Even snakes, you won't find them here."'

He grinned. 'That's what I thought. Lie down on the floor. I have an idea.'

The walls of the old shop were a dirty beige, but Ben guessed that they'd once been painted with white limewash. He broke off a corner of the crate and used it to scrape off a teaspoonful of chalky powder, which he daubed carefully onto Martine's face. Soon she was vampire white.

'The same colour as Mr Rat,' Ben teased, earning himself a hard slap for his cheek.

After checking through the vent that Griffin's companions were still asleep, he knocked and called 'Help!' just loud enough to attract their leader's attention.

'What do want?' Griffin growled through the door. 'Do you think this is a hotel where you can order breakfast?'

'Griffin, this is an emergency,' Ben said. 'Martine is ill.'

'I don't believe you,' came the response. 'It's a trick so you can get away. Don't worry; we're not going to hurt you. We will let you go when we find the leopard.'

'Griffin, what if something happens to her? Do you really want that on your conscience?'

There was a long pause and then a key scraped in the lock and the rusty metal door screeched open a crack. Griffin peered suspiciously into the storeroom. His eyes were bloodshot and he smelled of beer. When he caught sight of Martine lying white and prone on the concrete, he was aghast.

'Heh!' he exclaimed, stepping into the room and locking the door behind him. 'What has happened here? What is wrong with her?'

'She's hypoglycaemic,' Ben said gravely. 'Her blood sugar has gone down. She urgently needs some form of liquid sugar, like a sweet fizzy drink or even just some sugar in water. If she has that, she will be fine. Otherwise . . . '

'Otherwise what will happen?'

'I'm not exactly sure,' Ben said. 'But it'll probably be bad.'

On cue, Martine writhed on the floor and made a choking noise.

'Mwali, don't desert us now,' Griffin cried. He unlocked the door. 'We have a bottle of cream soda but we have no fridge so it is warm. Would that be okay?'

Ben gave him a winning smile. 'Warm cream soda would be perfect.'

Half an hour later, he and Martine were cantering towards the granite mountain where Martine had first encountered Khan. A leadrope tied to her saddle forced Mambo to keep up with Sirocco.

Martine could not get over the genius of Ben's escape plan, or his audacity in pulling in off. He'd not lost his cool for a second. 'But what made you think of it?' she said, slowing the horses to give them a breather. 'What made you think of the Enemy of Lions?'

'Easy,' he said. 'An ant crawled over my foot when I was sitting on the floor and it made me think that if there were ordinary ants in our cell, there might also be the biting kind. I thought how brilliant it would be if the Enemies of Lions could be turned into the Enemies of Leopard Hunters.'

Martine giggled at the memory. 'Boy, did they ever.'

After Griffin had brought the cream soda in a plastic cup, 'Just in case you get any wrong ideas', Ben had sent him away, explaining that Martine needed to be kept very quiet, but that he'd let him know how she was doing very shortly. He'd poured a trail of the green fizzy drink from the waterpipe to the door, then sprinkled the remainder over the sacks they'd slept on, leaving a corner of each dry.

Lured by the sugar, a thick black column of the ants was soon marching out through the pipe, down the wall and along the floor to the threshold. The sacks became shimmering black rectangles of massed ant armies. Holding the dry corners, Ben pushed them carefully behind the wooden crate.

When he judged there were enough of them, he summoned Griffin again. Martine, who'd wiped the paint dust off her face and pinched her cheeks so she looked flushed, pretended to be revived and ready to at least discuss helping to find the leopard if it would mean he would let them go sooner. Her job was to keep Griffin standing on the threshold long enough for the Enemies of Lions to make their way up his trouser leg.

Their plan came close to failing. Once Griffin was satisfied that Martine was once again in possession of her powers, he wanted to leave right away. Martine had to fake a sudden relapse to keep him in the room. Ben used the distraction to flick the dregs of the cream soda onto Griffin's shoe in the hope that it would encourage the ants to make the climb up his leg.

Seconds later, Griffin let out a tormented scream. He unlocked the storeroom door and went tearing out into the overcast morning. He was leaping, twisting and screeching like a madman. His friends sat up, bleary-eyed. As soon as they saw the storeroom door open, the keys swinging in the lock, they came barrelling towards it, but Martine and Ben were ready with the sacks. A single swish sent showers of biting ants all over the men. They ripped off their shirts, shouting and cursing, and went tearing into the bush after Griffin. None of them were in any condition to prevent their prisoners' getaway.

Now Martine and Ben were racing to try to reach Khan, not knowing if the hunters had got there first. A pair of Black Eagles and a few vultures was circling the granite mountain where Martine had initially encountered him and she feared the worst, but Ben insisted that birds of prey often hovered in the vicinity of hunts, knowing there might be easy pickings.

They were trotting again when Odilo suddenly came rushing out of the bush, his mournful face transformed by a smile. Sirocco shied again, but this time Martine was ready for her and barely lost her seat.

'Please, my friends, you must go to Black Eagle Lodge straight away,' he said, reaching up to give them each an African handshake. 'Straight away. Ngwenya came to our village with your grandmother and Sadie not even one hour past. They are searching for you.'

'My grandmother and Sadie are at the retreat?' Martine cried. 'That's fantastic. Are they all right? Have the charges been dropped?'

'Yes,' said Odilo, 'but they are very frightened because we had to tell them we had not seen you both since yesterday. Ngwenya is too much upset. He is very cross with himself for not accompanying you to the village. He is searching for you in the hills. Where have you been?'

As thrilled as she was to hear that her grandmother was at the retreat and unharmed, Martine was aware that every second was precious if she and Ben were to get to

Khan in time. She gave a sketchy account of their night at the hands of Griffin and his friends, leaving out the part about the Enemies of Lions. The details would keep for another day.

Odilo's expression resumed its customary mournfulness. 'I'm sorry for this,' he said. 'My son, even as a small boy he was very, very smart. For many years he dreamed of going to university to be a lawyer. But after school he met these *tsotsis* and they turned his head with stories of the life he will have if he finds this treasure. Now all he can talk about is gold, gold, gold. I tell him, "Griffin, no good can come of this. It will end with you crying in jail."'

He looked up at Martine. 'I'm sorry for what he did to you, especially after you gave us the *muti* that made our daughter well again.'

Gunshots rang out in the distance. Sirocco danced skittishly and pawed at the ground. There was a knot of panic in Martine's throat as she tried to control the Arab.

Ben urged Mambo up beside her. 'We need to go,' he said.

'Yes,' agreed Odilo, misunderstanding, 'you must get back to Gogo and your grandmother at Black Eagle.'

'Sorry, Odilo,' said Martine. 'We can't until we've found Khan. We have to try to save him from Mr Rat's hunters.'

Odilo couldn't believe what he was hearing. 'This is madness,' he protested. 'Mr Ratcliffe and his hunters, these are very dangerous men. This is something for the police. Please, children, you must get home to Gogo and your granny. Come, let me go with you.'

Martine's chin was set with determination. 'Tell my grandmother that I love her and can't wait to see her. Tell her that I hope she understands why we can't come back just yet. Right now we have a promise to keep.'

18

It was the witchdoctor who told them they were too late.

They came cantering out of the bush in a headlong rush and were confronted with a sight so surreal that it was too much even for Mambo. He slammed on brakes and Ben sailed over his head, fortunately landing agilely on his feet. Sirocco reared and threatened to bolt, and Martine had to dismount in order to calm her. Then she and Ben stood transfixed by the bizarre, almost mystical scene before them.

Beneath a low, charcoal sky was a ring of ten vultures. With their hunched shoulders, grey crests and shifty, all-knowing eyes, they resembled judges – spiteful, bad-tempered judges, going by the way they were hissing, cawing and pecking at each other over something unseen. In the centre of the circle, wearing his necklace of horns, belt of ostrich feathers and leopard-skin kilt, was the witchdoctor.

Martine jolted herself out of her trance and moved forward. Ben was close behind her. She stopped so suddenly that Ben ran into her. At the witchdoctor's feet was a sticky pool of blood, buzzing with flies.

'You have come too late,' he said. 'The leopard has been shot with the Rat Man's bullet.' He put a hand close to his heart to demonstrate where the lethal bullet had struck. An odour of alcohol drifted in Martine and Ben's direction.

'No!' cried Martine in anguish. 'He can't be dead. He just can't. I promised him I would save him.'

'I don't believe it,' said Ben. 'It's too quiet. If the leopard were dead, the hunters would be celebrating. There would be drag marks from where they loaded his body onto their jeep. And the vultures would not be here. They'd be circling the area where his carcass was, possibly even the jeep.'

The witchdoctor waved his arms and the vultures lifted screaming into the air, a sinister cloud of beating, dark wings. They settled in the tops of the peeling plain trees nearby, watching and waiting.

'I did not say he was dead,' he told Ben a little irritably. 'But he is dying. He has run for his life with the hunters behind him. Soon those who want Lobengula's treasure will be chasing him too.'

'Can you help us?' Martine begged. 'Can you throw the bones and tell us how we might get to him before they do?'

The witchdoctor gave a harsh chuckle. 'You shame me in front of my tribe; in front of people who believe that I am the best healer in Zimbabwe. You make me look like a fool, and now you expect me to assist you. You are dreaming, child. Go back to your *sangoma* friend and ask her. See if she can tell you where the leopard is.'

'Firstly, I didn't shame you,' Martine said angrily. 'You brought shame on yourself. Before you came, Mercy told us that you were the most talented traditional healer in Zimbabwe. You could have at least stayed sober until after you'd treated her sick child. You made the choice to drink and behave like a fool.

'As for my friend, Grace, if she was here, she *would* be able to tell me where the leopard is. But she's a few thousand miles away and you're right here. I don't know what Griffin bribed you with to make you tell him that the leopard needed to be dead before he could find the treasure, although I can guess. It doesn't matter. What's done is done. You have a chance to make things right. Are you going to take it?'

For a moment, the only sound was the eerie cries of the disgruntled vultures. Martine began to take in the enormity of what she'd done. She'd read the riot act to one of the most powerful figures in the Matopos and now there could be hell to pay.

She glanced at Ben and he was staring at her in

amazement. The witchdoctor, who at the beginning of her speech had produced a brown bottle from the depths of his kilt and was in the midst of taking a swig, flung it away from him. It hit a rock and shattered. A clear liquid gushed out.

'There are many curses I could put on you for saying these things,' he said quietly. 'You received my warning this morning, I am sure. But you have spoken the truth in the way that only an outsider could. It is painful for me to hear and it is shameful, but I cannot deny it. This thing, this *poison*, has a hold over me and I have found no herb, no plant, which can cure me. It is like a python around my neck, strangling me. Men such as Griffin have been feeding that python, bringing me these brown bottles so that I might help them with their wicked quest. I have been too weak to resist.'

'Is there anyone you would trust to help you?' Ben asked. 'Anyone you could talk to.'

The witchdoctor didn't seem to hear him. He removed his ceremonial pouch, stepped away from the buzzing patch of red and faced Martine. 'You humiliated me in front of my tribe and I will not soon forget it,' he said. 'But I will also remember something else. If it were not for you and your *sangoma*'s *muti* the baby might have died.'

'I would never have known Grace's medicine would help Emelia if you hadn't said the name of the plant.' Martine said graciously. Her rage had subsided and, after his courage in admitting that his addiction was squeezing the life from him, she felt an urge to comfort him.

The witchdoctor shook his head. 'I will throw the bones and tell you what you need to know. Perhaps there is still time for you to save your friend.'

He squatted and began chanting to himself, though whether it was in Ndebele or some ancient African language they couldn't tell. His rough hands, like the parched skin of an elephant, scattered the bones onto the dry earth. Martine tried her hardest to visualize Khan safe and well and happy, and once again she saw him on a mountainside at Sawubona, golden and whole.

The witchdoctor looked up from his bones. 'The one who reads the sign best will find the leopard first.'

'Oh,' said Ben.

That's not particularly helpful, thought Martine.

But the witchdoctor hadn't finished. He addressed them both, but his eyes were on Martine. 'You are bound together but you will be torn apart. When that happens, look to the House of Bees.'

19

'That's not a lot to go on, especially if we have to interpret the sign before the hunters do,' said Martine, urging Sirocco forward. She was finding it hard not to panic at the thought of Khan's life ebbing away. 'They have a head start.'

'It's not a lot to go on,' agreed Ben. He was leaning down from his saddle, scanning the ground for tracks or spots of blood as they went. 'But he did tell us something that could prove vital. He said we'd be torn apart. Now that we know that, maybe we can prevent it.'

Martine had a flashback to her conversation with Grace before she left Sawubona, the one where she'd said that if the San had only made her destiny clearer in their paintings she could have avoided all the bad stuff.

'We can try,' she said to Ben, 'but I don't think it really works that way. Grace says that if a person could see their future, they'd "only choose the good stuff, the easy stuff". They'd never learn from their mistakes and never experience the important things in life because they're usually the hardest things. But I do think it's a bit weird that both Grace and the witchdoctor talked about us being bound together. What do you think the witchdoctor meant when he said "Look to the House of Bees"?'

'I don't know,' Ben said absently. They had reached a stretch of bare rock leading down to a river, a tracker's biggest challenge. 'Maybe we're meant to look for a beehive, or maybe it's the name of a local house or even a hill?'

He got off Mambo. It took several minutes of casting around before a trace of sand in a crevice of the rock revealed a partial boot-print. A little way on he found a smear of blood.

'They're right behind him,' he said. 'I wish Tendai was here. He has such an amazing eye for this. It's going to take me years to learn even half of what he knows about tracking.'

Martine was on tenterhooks. She was worried about what would happen if they didn't find the leopard, but she was even more afraid of what would happen if they did. When she'd had to rescue Jemmy, she'd done so knowing that he was a gentle, beautiful creature who would never harm her. She and Ben hadn't thought through the rescue of Khan in any way. If he were wounded he would be lashing out at everyone and everything. He'd be more likely to bite her head off than lie around waiting for her to summon up her gift.

Ben was at the river's edge. 'Martine, it looks like Khan and the hunters have crossed here. We should probably go on foot.'

Martine opened her mouth to say that the best thing they could do was race back to Black Eagle and get Sadie and her grandmother to call the police. But that would take hours. No, she and Ben would have to press on and hope for the best.

'All right,' she said, putting a hand on her survival pouch to check that it was fastened securely. 'Let's give the horses a drink of water and tie them up in the shade.'

It was easy for Ben to track the men across the river, because their boots had left bits of mud drying on the flat rocks on the other side. But where the grass began, there was a problem. There were two faint leopard paw prints heading southwest, one smudged and slightly twisted, but then, inexplicably, they vanished. It was as if Khan had been plucked into the heavens. The hunters had obviously spent a considerable time searching the area for some trace of him, before setting off in the direction that the leopard had last been taking.

Ben lingered by the riverbank.

'Let's go, Ben,' Martine said impatiently. 'We're going to have to run for a while or at least jog if we're going to overtake the hunters.'

He stood without moving. 'Something's wrong. The locals believe that after even every leopard in Zimbabwe is gone, Khan will survive; that he'll be the last leopard. They believe it because he's so cunning. Remember what I told you about Tendai's theory that people crossing rivers unconsciously walking in the direction they intend to travel, even if they're trying not to?'

'That's people,' Martine said. 'Surely a leopard's not capable of thinking like that?'

'Maybe not. But we already know that Khan is no ordinary leopard. His tracks show him heading southwest as he crosses the river and then when they appear again he's going due south. What if he doubled back? What if he had the wit to jump onto the rock from the path, which would explain the way his claws seemed to have dug into the ground, and then he waded along the river for a while.'

Martine was frantic, but she knew that all the rushing in the world wouldn't help if they misread the sign and ended up in the wrong place. 'Okay,' she said. 'It's worth a try.'

Ten minutes later, Ben gave a triumphant shout. He'd found a series of upturned pebbles on the riverbank, about fifty yards along from where they'd started, their undersides black and moist from the wet clay. 'That shows they've recently been turned,' he explained to Martine.

Next he spotted a ball of bloodstained cobwebs that had been wiped from a bush. From then on, they moved very quickly. After leaving the river, the leopard had started to bleed profusely and tracking him, at least to Ben's sharp eyes, was simply a matter of following the trail of blood. Ben jogged swiftly through the bush with Martine struggling to keep up. She could only just make out his blue T-shirt and jeans through the trees when she heard him shout, 'Martine, I think he's up here. Isn't this Rock Rabbit Hill – the one Ngwenya told us about?'

A hand was clapped over her mouth. There was a faint smell of cologne mingled with tripe. Griffin! He pulled her off the path and into a ditch, making almost no sound.

On the path ahead, Ben tensed when Martine didn't answer. He spun round. 'Martine? Martine!'

He guessed immediately that she'd been snatched or worse. He sprinted back down the path and began studying the ground where he'd last seen her. So absorbed was he in his task that he didn't see the hunters until he almost walked into them.

'What an unexpected pleasure,' drawled the duty manager from the Lazy J sourly, his bushy blond moustache twitching. He was with one of the guides who'd surrounded Ben and Martine in the forest.

Ben could still have made a break for it, but he didn't want to go anywhere until he knew where Martine was or if the hunters themselves had taken her.

'Where's your girlfriend?' the duty manager demanded in the next breath, answering one of Ben's questions at least. 'I have a score to settle with her.'

'I think she has a few to settle with you,' Ben replied coolly. 'Unfortunately, she's not here at the moment. She's at Black Eagle Lodge with her grandmother, and the police are on their way to arrest you for trespassing.'

The duty manager laughed. 'The police here are in the pay of Mr Ratcliffe whom you've grievously offended. If I were you I wouldn't count on them to come riding in like knights on white chargers. They know we're here. Now I'm going to ask you for the last time. Where's your girlfriend? What were you yelling just now – Mary?'

'If you're talking about my friend, her name is Susan,' Ben said. 'And like I told you, she's back at the retreat. I was calling for Mrs Scott's dog, Magnus. Maggy, I call him.'

In the ditch nearby, Martine listened in horror. If Griffin hadn't been holding her in such a vicelike grip, she would have burst from the ditch and confronted the hunters, regardless of the outcome.

'You're a terrible liar,' the duty manager told Ben, 'and if you continue to lie you're going to make me lose my temper.'

Ben folded his arms. 'Well, you're just going to have to lose it, then. If you think I'm lying, why don't you try to find Susan yourself? I mean, can you see her anywhere?'

'No,' admitted the hunter. 'But then I don't see your dog around either.'

'That's because he ran away when he saw the leopard,' Ben told him.

'The leopard!' cried the guide. 'Where is the leopard?'

'The leopard you shot?' Ben said. 'Do you really think I'm going to tell you where he's gone so you can finish him off? Anyway, they're expecting me back at Black Eagle. I need to go.'

The guide lifted his rifle menacingly. 'You're not going anywhere. You're going to show us where the leopard is hiding.'

'And why in the world would I want to do that?' said Ben.

'Ernest, put down the gun and stop acting like a gangster,' the duty manager ordered gruffly. 'Look, kid, you might not be aware of it but there's a bounty on the leopard's head. A thousand dollars dead or alive. It's yours if you can lead us to him.'

Ben grinned. 'In that case, follow me.'

20

Griffin waited until the only sound was the cooing of a lone dove before taking his hand from Martine's mouth and pushing her none too gently out of the ditch. He'd taken off his white shirt and hat and was wearing his soiled black waistcoat and trousers. His face, neck and bare arms were covered in swollen ant bites. He looked like the victim of some ghastly disease.

'You are lucky to have such a good friend,' he said. 'Loyal friends who will stand by you no matter what, those are hard to come by these days.'

'Yeah, well, maybe if you'd gone to law school like your father says you wanted to, instead of hanging about with lowlifes looking for gold and diamonds which doesn't belong to you, you might have met those kind of friends,' Martine responded coldly.

'Papa remembered my dream?' Griffin said. A wistful expression flickered across his face, but then he shook himself and scowled. 'You are too young to know anything about life. It is not always easy.'

He gave her a shove. 'I was very prepared to be nice to you and your friend, but you tricked me and caused me to be attacked by the Enemy of Lions. Have you felt their bites? It is like being pierced by needles made red-hot in fire. So now you have two choices. You are going to help me, or you are going to pay. The leopard has been shot and the witchdoctor says it is dying. Perhaps it is dead already. You will use your gift to locate Khan. Before the sun sets, the prophecy will be fulfilled. In the last resting place of the king of leopards I will find the king's treasure.'

'The witchdoctor told you that?' Martine felt a sense of disappointment. She'd really believed that he might change.

'No,' replied Griffin. 'I tried to give the stubborn old drunk some wine in payment for a prediction, but he smashed it against a rock and became very abusive. He said that the leopard was dying and I was wasting my time. Luckily I found your footprints down by the river and followed you here.'

He jerked her arm. 'Come, let's go. Let's find the leopard.'

Martine took a couple of steps along the path taken by

Ben and the hunters, but Griffin wrenched her back so brutally that she winced in pain.

'No more tricks,' he shouted. 'I heard your friend telling you that the leopard is on Rock Rabbit Hill. Start walking.'

The climb to the top of the fortress of rocks was agony for Martine. She was tired, hungry and thirsty, and with every arduous step she expected to come across the bloody body of Khan and to have to deal with Griffin tossing it aside to scrabble for the king's treasure.

She tried to think of an escape plan but her brain was like cotton wool. She didn't even have the energy to sneak a hand into her survival kit – not that there was anything in it that could help her at this moment. And besides, Griffin was right on her heels. The witchdoctor's words kept running through her head. 'You are bound together but you will be torn apart. When that happens, look to the House of Bees.'

'*What* House of Bees?' Martine thought frustratedly.

A police siren wailed in the distance. It was so unexpected that Griffin, in mid-stride between two rocks, lost his footing and slipped.

Martine seized the opportunity to make a run for it. Somehow she had to get to the top of the hill and signal the distant police car. It was her only hope. Up she went, forcing one exhausted leg in front of the other. Griffin came scrambling after her. Martine felt like she sometimes did in dreams, when she was being pursued by some unknown assailant and her legs refused to work.

In seconds, Griffin would grab her and this time there would be no Khan, Ben or Ngwenya to save her. The sweat ran into her eyes, stinging them and blurring her vision. Through a red haze, she saw a swollen dark mass suspended from a tree. Black specks circled it.

The House of Bees!

Martine scooped up a rock as she ran and threw it with all her might. The rock hit the bees' nest square on. It vibrated crazily – the black cloud of bees vibrating with it, hung momentarily suspended, and then plunged to earth.

The swarm swerved towards her with a hum so loud it resonated in her chest like a bass drum. Martine threw herself on the ground and lay motionless. There was a rush of whirring air as the bees swept over her, followed by a strangled yell as they descended upon Griffin. He turned and fled down the mountainside.

Martine got to her feet, swaying and stumbled on. Her sole intention was to make it to the top of the hill, where she could more easily be seen. She was almost there when she stepped on a piece of honeycomb. It stuck to her shoe. She paused to detach it and that's when it happened.

That's when the ground gave way beneath her feet.

Her stomach was left behind, and she was falling, falling, falling, an avalanche of earth falling with her. Each time she thought she'd reached the bottom, the bottom would give way and she'd fall again.

When she did hit the ground it was with a nasty crunch, and yet still the avalanche kept coming. Moist, cool earth – earth that smelled of worms and rotting leaves – was filling her mouth, eyes and ears, and as fast as she tried to spit it out or push it away, more came in. She was choking on it. She couldn't breathe.

Seconds before the last chink of daylight was erased she saw Khan. He was trying to get to her through the debris, although whether he wanted to save her or attack her, she didn't know. She just knew she was about to be buried alive.

Quite suddenly, everything was black and still. The roof stopped falling and she could breathe again. Gingerly, she tested her limbs. They were sore, but it didn't feel as if anything was broken. Not yet at least. But who knew what Khan had in mind. Maybe he'd just chew her up whole. She strained her ears. Was he readying himself to pounce? She unzipped her survival kit and groped inside for her torch.

It was gone.

Disbelief and a panic so extreme she felt as if she'd been stabbed in the stomach, hit Martine like a tidal wave. This couldn't be happening. Through every adventure and every near-death disaster she'd experienced since arriving in Africa, she'd been kept going by the knowledge that there were tools in her survival kit that could save her. But it wasn't only about what was in the pouch. It was that everything in it had been given to her by someone she cared for – by the

Morrisons back in England, by Grace, Tendai, Gwyn Thomas and even by Caracal Junior's most infuriating boy, Claudius. Now it was almost empty.

Martine couldn't understand it. The survival kit had been with her nearly every minute, apart from a few hours the previous night when she'd forgotten it by the fire after the crisis with baby Emelia. It was hard to believe that her pink torch, Swiss Army knife and other items could have held any interest for the weary villagers. Then who? The witchdoctor? She doubted it. The dogs? A roaming night animal?

A picture of fluttering eyelashes and a long yellow beak popped into Martine's head. 'Magnus!' she gasped.

The irony of it was too cruel. She'd escaped the human treasure seekers, only to be robbed by a treasure seeking bird, and now she was alone in the blackness with the most dangerous animal on earth: a wounded leopard.

21

Khan gave a menacing growl that was somehow magnified by the dead air and the blinding dark. Martine tried to curl herself into a small ball. If she could have seen his eyes she could have attempted to use her gift to stop him from attacking her, but without light she could do nothing.

Without changing position, she opened the pouch again and rummaged through it in case it contained some life-saving device she'd somehow missed. But it was empty apart from Grace's headache potion and a tube of superglue. The hornbill had done a pretty thorough job of nicking the shiny things. Oddly, it was still quite heavy, which was why Martine hadn't noticed the missing items sooner. She unzipped an interior pocket she rarely used and her fingers touched something hard and smooth. Something waxy. Candles! And, behind them, slightly crushed, was the box of matches. She and Ben had taken them, along with one or two other supplies, as they left the house and she'd put them into her survival pouch without thinking.

She couldn't hear Khan, but sensed he was very near. It would have been comforting to think that he could see as little as she did, but she knew leopards were nocturnal and had perfect night vision. In all probability, he was watching her every move.

Striking a match, she held it to the candlewick. Khan snarled at the sizzle and the flare of yellow light. As she'd suspected, he was very close to her, but he wasn't poised to pounce. He was in a smooth hollow on the rock floor of a long cavern. His ribcage was rising and falling very rapidly and his breathing was distressed. She soon saw why. A pool of treacly blood had collected around his chest, staining his golden fur scarlet. A gaping wound was the source of it.

Martine's eyes filled with tears. She forgot to be afraid, forgot that he was a killer, forgot everything except that she'd promised to protect him and failed.

'Khan,' she whispered, 'I'm sorry.'

Khan's eyes were glazed with pain. He rose with effort and wandered unsteadily over to a shadowed area. Martine lifted the candle so that the wobbly circle of light illuminated him. He was lapping at a tiny spring.

Judging from the watermarks on the smooth rocks that surrounded it, it had once been the source of a large stream – perhaps even an underground river – but it had dried up over the years and was little more than a trickle.

The leopard drank for a long time, and then he returned to the hollow and lay down again. Blood leaked steadily onto the floor beneath his chest. He growled softly to himself and licked hopelessly at his scarlet paws.

Martine was in despair. It was agony to see such a proud, magnificent animal reduced to a pitiful invalid. She was sure that if he carried on losing blood at the present rate he would die within the hour.

Since he was too preoccupied with his own suffering to pose a threat, Martine climbed stiffly to her feet and began to take stock of their surroundings. It didn't take long to establish that their situation was desperate. The cavern they were in seemed to be the end of a tunnel hewn by the water and now blocked by an immense boulder. Martine tried holding the candle to the hole where the spring flowed out but couldn't see what was on the other side. Whether the boulder was part of the landslide or had been there for centuries was difficult to tell.

She checked the cavern roof but that didn't look hopeful either. The hole through which she'd fallen was also blocked, and was much too high for her to reach even if it wasn't. It's not as if there was a chair or a ladder she could use to stand on. Last she examined the walls. They were solid rock. Or at least she thought they were. There was something subtly different about the wall behind the leopard. She stared at it for a long time but couldn't work out what.

Realistically her, and Khan's, only chance of survival was to be saved by someone on the outside. Problem was, nobody knew they were there. She could try shouting, but it was hard to believe that anyone would hear her.

Martine wanted to cry. Some of the ordeals she'd faced over the past eight months had been so horrific she'd been quite sure that if she lived through them she'd never experience anything worse. And yet here she was, buried alive with a wounded leopard. 'You couldn't make it up,' she said out loud and very nearly managed a smile.

She eyed the bleeding leopard, sniffed loudly, and pulled herself together. Tendai was always telling her that the more hopeless things seemed in a survival situation, the more you had to focus on doing what you could do, minute by minute. And what she needed to do now was help the leopard.

Her priority was to stop him bleeding. But how? She was in a solid rock cavern with a virtually empty survival kit. And yet Tendai and Grace insisted that even the most barren places had something to offer in terms of healing herbs or tools that could save a life.

'When you have looked with your own eyes and you can't see anything to help you, that's when you must look with the eyes of a Bushman or an animal,' Tendai would say. 'The San lived in the deserts of the Kalahari where you or I would see nothing but sand. But they found every medicine they needed and all the food they could eat.'

Martine tried looking around the cave with San eyes. The only natural resource there was water. She didn't know how clean it was, but animals have very good instincts about such things and the fact that Khan had drunk so much of it was a positive sign. Water on its own was not going to be much use, but if the spring had ever been exposed to sunlight there might be moss. And Grace had taught her that moss was almost as effective as gauze dressing when it came to wounds.

She carried the candle over to the thin stream, keeping a wary eye on Khan. Worryingly, he didn't even lift his head. Martine knew that his condition was getting critical. She sighed with relief when she saw the luxuriant bed of green growing up on the far side of the water. Using a sharp triangle of broken rock, she cut two square mats of nature's best field dressing.

It was her first breakthrough.

All she had to do now was find some form of antiseptic or antibiotic. Would Grace's headache potion be any use?

She went over to examine her survival kit again and noticed that the bottom of her right shoe kept sticking to the floor. That reminded her that she'd stepped on some honeycomb shortly before her fall. Honey! Honey was an excellent natural antibiotic and wound healer. What if the chunk of honeycomb had tumbled with her? That would make all the difference.

She rushed over to the pile of earth and stones and scrabbled at it like a terrier after a bone. Thanks to its stickiness, she found the honeycomb almost immediately. She rinsed it clean and ate a few chunks to give her energy. It had a rich toffee taste, which boosted her spirits. They needed boosting. The hard part was still to come.

Khan's head rested on the worn hollow of rock with a familiarity that made Martine wonder if he came here often; if this was his secret lair. She'd assumed that he'd tumbled through the cavern ceiling like she had, but if this was his secret den he must have been here already. And if that was true, a landslide must have sealed the tunnel *after* he was inside.

Sensing he was the object of her attention, Khan gave a warning snarl so vicious Martine's heart almost leapt from her chest. Her only consolation was that he'd had two previous opportunities to hurt her and hadn't. On the second occasion, he'd actually saved her from Mr Rat and his thugs.

Martine decided that the only solution was to pretend that the leopard was just an oversized version of Shelby and Warrior, her grandmother's cats. She picked up the moss, honey and her almost empty survival kit, marched purposefully over to him, and sat down beside him as if she dealt with injured leopards every day of the week.

In the flickering candlelight, the expression on Khan's face was priceless. Had his condition not been so serious, Martine would have dissolved into giggles. He looked too shocked to object. He lay on his side and, for once, was quite docile.

Before he had time to change his mind, Martine pressed the moss to the wound on his chest, earning a savage growl for her bravery but nothing worse. Her other hand covered his heart. She closed her eyes. Nearly two months had passed since she'd last drawn on her gift and she was not entirely confident it would work, but she focussed on Khan's silken fur beneath her palms and the steady *doof, doof, doof* beat of his heart. Her hands grew hotter. Flashes of light and memory, like incoming pictures on a faulty television, began to crash around her head.

She saw the faces of the ancients, the San people, and somehow they were kinder and wiser than she could ever have imagined, and they were chanting with her, encouraging her, and it seemed to Martine that they were speaking in the language that the witchdoctor had used and that she could understand it. A magical energy came from them and passed through her as if she were a lightning conductor.

At first the leopard writhed beneath her touch as if her hands were so hot they were singeing him, but gradually his muscles relaxed and a peace came over him. She opened her eyes and lifted away the moss. The bleeding had stopped. Using her hankerchief as a wet cloth, she rinsed shrapnel from the wound and wiped the area around it. Then she dribbled honey onto the exposed flesh.

Throughout this process Khan lay still, although he trembled slightly. Once the blood had been cleaned away Martine was pleased to see the bullet hole wasn't as wide or deep as she'd feared. It had bled a lot, but the wound itself was clean. That meant she could use superglue to close it. A long time ago she'd employed soldier termites to stitch up a fallen kudu, but Grace had wisely pointed out they weren't always going to be handy and that the glue would be a worthwhile addition to her survival kit.

'I would have thought that you'd prefer to use something more natural than hardware-store glue to treat wounds,' Martine had said.

'T'aint about what's natural, honey,' Grace had replied. 'It's about what *works*.'

The superglue also meant that no termites were decapitated in the process of stitching, which was definitely good. And it was more efficient. Martine squeezed a minute amount along one edge of the wound and pressed the two sides together. It sealed perfectly.

By now she felt confident enough in Khan to pour Grace's painkilling potion into the side of his mouth. He licked his lips and wrinkled up his nose, baring his fearsome teeth. It was obvious he loathed the foul taste, but he seemed to understand it was for his own good.

With the immediate crisis over, Martine realized how shattered she was. As long as she'd been focussed on Khan, she hadn't had time to think about herself. Now she couldn't stop shaking. She washed her hands and face in the spring. The thing she kept thinking about was what would happen if nobody found them. What if this cold cavern was to become their tomb?

As far as she could tell, she'd done everything she could for the moment. She had light and food (well, a few tablespoons' worth of honey) and they both had water. Water could keep them alive for weeks, although if nobody found them that might not necessarily be a good thing. They'd simply starve to death over a longer period. What's worse, they'd starve to death in the dark. There were only two candles in the survival kit and the first one was half gone.

She wondered how Ben was doing. He'd protected her from the hunters at great risk to himself, but she had a feeling he would have outsmarted them or, at the very least, outrun them. With any luck the police siren she'd heard belonged to a squad car full of good police, rather than corrupt police, who'd rescue Ben from the clutches of the Rat's men and then start combing the hills for her and Khan.

She thought, too, about her grandmother, who she hoped was not too distressed about her disappearance; about Jemmy, who she missed with every fibre of her being; Grace, who would be proud of how she'd used the knowledge she'd been give to heal the leopard; Tendai, whose bushcraft lessons had helped her think her way through the situation methodically when a lot of kids she knew would have been hysterical with despair; and, of course, her mum and dad, who might be gone but were always with her and watching over her, every minute of every day.

Her watch showed that it was early evening, but time was meaningless in the cavern. Martine propped herself up against the cold rock wall and tried to doze. She was as scared to blow out the candle and face the suffocating darkness as she was to keep it burning and see it melt away to nothing. She would keep it lit until she felt sleepier. It gave the illusion of warmth. The temperature in the cave was dropping by the minute.

Martine looked longingly at the leopard's golden form. She wondered if he was as scared and lonely as she was. She tried to remind herself that leopards were the most unpredictable and fierce of the big cats and that he was unlikely to be feeling any such thing, but she had very little to lose.

She went over to him and lay down in the hollow. It was strangely soft, almost cushioned. Khan half-opened one eye but did nothing to suggest he minded. Heart pounding, Martine blew out the candle and snuggled against his silky back, carefully avoiding his wound. When he didn't react, she put an arm over him and rested her palm on one of his great paws, feeling the sharpness of his claws and the heat of his rough, fleshy pads.

She was just dozing off when he began to purr – big, tractor-type purrs that vibrated through them both. A slow grin spread across Martine's face.

It was a strange kind of heaven, sleeping with a wild leopard, but it was heaven nonetheless.

22

*T*uk-tuk-tuk. *Tat-tat-tat. Tuk-tuk-tuk. Tat-tat-tat.*
'Magnus, leave me alone,' grumbled Martine. 'It's
too early. I've told you before not to wake me at the crack
of dawn.'

She stretched stiffly and her arm touched something
soft and silky. It let out a noise that was somewhere
between a growl and a purr. Martine sat bolt upright in
the darkness. The terror of the previous day came back
to her. She was hundreds of feet underground with the
world's biggest leopard and they were in a cave that
could soon become their tomb.

She groped about for the candle and matches and the

cavern filled with light. Khan sat up too and his yellow eyes swung on her like headlamps. The hatred she'd once seen in them had been replaced with a look that definitely wasn't love, but wasn't far from it either. She leaned forward without fear and examined his chest wound. There was hardly any swelling and the tissue around it was pink and healthy. Martine felt quite pleased with her handiwork. 'Not bad for an amateur,' she boasted to Khan, and ran her hand over his amazing spotted coat.

The leopard gave a blood-curdling snarl and surged to his feet. Martine froze. Was she about to pay the price for crossing a line with him? Was he going to turn on her? Then she heard it again – a faint knocking.

Khan moved on silent paws towards the centre of the cavern and crouched there, listening. The noise seemed to be coming from above. He looked round at Martine for reassurance.

'Maybe it's our friends,' Martine told him. 'Maybe they've found us. Maybe we're going to be saved.'

She was astonished to find that she experienced a slight twinge of sorrow at the thought. Of *course* she wanted to be rescued. Of *course* she wanted to see Ben and her grandmother and everyone else. But she also knew that the magic of this time with Khan, when it was just the two of them against the world and they were utterly dependant on one another, would never come again. As soon as anyone else entered the cavern, the specialness of these moments would be banished with the morning light.

Another more disturbing thought entered her head. What if the distant hammering wasn't her friends at all? What if it was Griffin and his crew wanting revenge, or Rex Ratcliffe's hunters, ready with their rifles? Those possibilities kept her from crying out for help. And yet anything must be better than starving to death in a black hole.

She got up from the hollow, thinking to herself that it had been surprisingly warm and comfortable for a rock bed. Too warm and comfortable. A ghost of an idea flitted across her mind, but it was gone before she could get a grip on it. The hammering outside had started again but it was not so loud. The rescue party was moving away.

Martine lifted the candle and was struck again by how the back wall of the cavern seemed slightly different to the rest. She rapped it with her knuckles to test it.

The elusive thought floated into her head. It had to do with a comment Ngwenya had made when he was telling them about Lobengula's treasure. He said that the burial party had 'hidden it well and sealed the entrance with a stone wall'.

Martine ran a hand over the wall, and that's when she knew. It was man-made! That's what was 'wrong' with it. Whoever had built it had done it superbly, going to enormous lengths to replicate exactly the colour and grain of the rock. Only someone who'd spent as much time in the cavern as she had would have noticed it was any different to the other walls.

The hairs stood up on the back of Martine's neck. She stared at the hollow. *The last resting place of the King of*

Leopards is the hiding place of the King's Treasure...

It wasn't the last resting place of the leopard, but it very nearly had been.

Khan was snarling at the boulder, his tail swishing furiously. He paced the cave on legs wobbly from blood loss. Martine thought she heard voices, but she was so preoccupied she dismissed it as being her imagination.

She bent down and studied the smooth impression in the cavern floor. It had a worn appearance which she'd put down to it having been used for months or even years as a sleeping area by Khan. But now she saw that it wasn't rock at all; it was ancient leather. She used the sharp piece of rock to prise up a corner. Underneath was a platform of wood, which was easy enough to lift off. And beneath that was a vault hewn from the rock. It was filled with dusty sacks and three rusty tins that might once have been silver. One of the sacks had a small rip in it, out of which protruded a single gold sovereign. It winked in the candlelight.

'Martine!' Ben's voice was muffled. 'Martine, are you in there? Oh, please be alive. MARTINE!'

As if in a dream, Martine replaced the wooden platform and the leather cover, went over to the pile of debris and used her sweatshirt to carry several loads to the hollow. She patted it down and put her sweatshirt on top of it. Then she walked slowly to Khan's side. She squatted down and put her arm around him.

'Ben! Ben, I'm here!' she shouted, and her voice echoed back at her, 'Ben-en-en-en! Ben-en-en-en, I'm here-ere-ere-ere!'

· 23 ·

M artine would always remember that day as one of the happiest and saddest ever. Happy because she and Khan were saved, and Ben, Sadie and her grandmother were in one piece, although all were a bit shaken. Happy too because there were lots of hugs and tears of joy, and because after the boulder had been pulled away from the tunnel entrance, she, her friends, and practically everyone from Mercy and Odilo's village had travelled to Black Eagle Lodge on the back of a tractor and trailer and enjoyed a celebration barbecue in the sunshine.

There was plenty to celebrate. A wave of arrests, for

starters. The District Attorney had been appalled to discover from Ngwenya that the involvement of several police officers in the pay of Rex Ratcliffe had led to the wrongful incarceration of two elderly women, one with a broken leg. He'd had his eye on the Lazy J for quite some time, and the evidence provided by the horse wrangler and the waiter finally gave him the ammunition he needed to get a search warrant. Not, however, before Sadie and Gwyn Thomas had spent a night in the cells with a host of petty thieves and one murderer.

'I haven't laughed so much in years,' declared Sadie, who seemed, bizarrely, to have relished the experience.

The District Attorney had taken a rather more dim view of his officers' conduct, and after a day of enquiries had banged them up in the same cells. The police car Martine had heard when she was fleeing Griffin belonged to constables sent from Bulawayo by the DA. They'd been on their way to arrest the hunters for trespassing and attempting to kill a protected animal without a licence. After they'd caught the duty manager chasing Ben with a stick, the policemen had added 'attempted assault' to the charge sheet.

On their way back to the retreat, they'd discovered a comatose figure by the roadside. It was Griffin, suffering an allergic reaction to the bee stings. He was so swollen that one of the constables described him as looking as if he'd been blown up with a bicycle pump. He'd been rushed to hospital and was sleeping off the medication. One of the first questions the police asked Martine was whether she and Ben wanted to press charges against the treasure seeker when he came to his senses. His *shamwaris* had fled the area and would have to be dealt with later.

After talking it over, Ben and Martine agreed not to press charges. The ants and bees had punished Griffin enough and they felt he'd probably learnt his lesson.

'Deep down, he's not a bad person,' Martine told Odilo. 'As you said, he's just fallen in with the wrong crowd and lost his way. If he gets a second chance, maybe he'll think about going back to school and ending up on the right side of the law.'

Rex Ratcliffe had been arrested for illegal hunting, foreign currency violations and other offences too numerous to list, and was likely to be in jail for quite some time. The Lazy J had been closed down with immediate effect, and all the animals were going to be re-homed in new sanctuaries.

'Good Rat-ence,' Sadie quipped when she was told about the Lazy J owner's grim future behind bars. She was full of smiles. On her release, she had checked her post office box in Bulawayo and found a heap of bookings from an American travel agent, plus a $1,000 cheque from an anonymous benefactor. It all meant that she could rehire her former Black Eagle staff, with one new addition: Odilo was to replace Sadie as chef.

'I don't have any imagination as a cook,' she admitted. 'The only recipes I know all seem to contain butternut squash.' But she was also beaming for another reason. 'I saw the leopard again,' she said over and over. 'I saw

Khan and he was worth every second of every day I spent fighting for him.'

Late afternoon, Martine and Ben climbed Elephant Rock and sat on the hill's summit watching the sun go down over the ancient landscape of the Matopos. They could see almost as far as the Hill of Benevolent Spirits and World's View. Magnus, the hornbill, had flown up with them and was perched on Martine's knee.

'Tell me again how you found me,' Martine said to Ben, unpacking the slices of chocolate cake she'd brought with her.

He stretched out his brown legs on the warm granite rock and ate a mouthful of cake before replying. 'Well, after the cops showed up and arrested the hunters, Ngwenya and I started searching for you. He's a pretty good tracker himself and between us we tracked you to the top of Rabbit Warren Hill. There your footprints just stopped. We could see that the ground near the tree had recently collapsed, as if there'd been a landslide or an old mine shaft had fallen in, and we were scared to death that you'd been buried alive, or were wandering around the catacomb of tunnels with concussion or even lying somewhere with a broken limb.'

He stopped. 'I was frightened I might never see you again.'

Martine grinned. 'You're not going to get rid of me that easily, you know.'

'Promise? Anyway, it took a long time to get a rescue effort together because it's impossible to dig up a whole hill and nobody could agree on where or how to start. If we'd got it wrong, we could have made things much worse for you. We needed equipment, a paramedic and a wildlife vet to tranquilize Khan if necessary. Plus your grandmother and Sadie wanted to be there, and most of the villagers insisted on helping.'

'It sounds as if it was one of those "too many cooks" situations,' Martine said sympathetically.

'It sort of was. Tribal custom meant that Chief Nyoni, who is the highest-ranking chief in the Matobo Hills, also had to be present. By coincidence, it turned out that his grandson was a famous wildlife vet. That was good news, but both of them were coming from different places and they took ages to arrive. It was very hard to be patient, but I just kept hoping that you'd figured out what the witchdoctor meant when he said, "Look to the House of Bees".'

Martine shuddered at the memory of the collective hum of the swarming bees. 'I did,' she said.

'We started digging at first light but we were getting nowhere fast,' Ben went on. 'Sadie and Mercy were waiting at the bottom because Sadie couldn't climb with her crutches and Mercy is ... well, Mercy is the wrong shape to clamber up mountains, and they kept shouting conflicting instructions. It was a bit annoying. But if it hadn't been for them and Magnus, we might never have found you.'

Martine stroked the hornbill's head and he swooned with delight. 'You're a bad bird for stealing my survival stuff, but I might have to forgive you,' she said. She took off her silver dolphin necklace and gave it to him. In a trice he'd scooped it into his yellow beak. 'Now we're connected, too,' she told him.

To Ben she said, 'So it was Mercy who noticed Magnus was behaving oddly?'

'Yes. She remarked to Sadie that it was weird how the hornbill kept flapping around this one shrub on the side of the hill. Sadie put two and two together and realized that Magnus might be trying to get to you. We pulled back the shrub to discover the old water tunnel, and the rest . . . '

'The rest is history,' finished Martine.

She knew the rest of the story off by heart. Ropes had been put around the boulder and the tunnel roof had been propped up with two big planks of wood in case it was unstable. Nobody, including Martine, knew how the leopard would react when the tunnel was cleared, so a decision was made that no more than four people would enter. At Martine's insistence, they were Ben, Ngwenya, Chief Nyoni, a frail, birdlike man, and the wildlife vet, Chief Nyoni's grandson. He'd travelled overnight from Hwange Game Reserve.

The vet was not able to approach Khan and had to examine him from the other side of the cavern, but he saw enough to be impressed that Martine had managed to stem the bleeding, and disinfect and seal the wound with only moss, honey and superglue to hand.

'All those years at veterinary school and I could have just stayed in the Matopos picking up tips from an eleven-year-old,' he joked.

After that, things got serious. Chief Nyoni sat Martine and Ben down and told them that late the previous night the leopard clan had gathered together to discuss Khan's future if he was found alive. Their number one priority was preserving Khan and his descendants for the benefit and enjoyment of future generations in the Matopos, and they agreed that if he had to be sent away to a place of safety for a few years until peace returned to Zimbabwe, then so be it. The following morning, they'd talked it over with Sadie and Gwyn Thomas, and the clan had unanimously agreed that if Khan survived he should go to live at Sawubona.

'Sawubona!' gasped Martine. 'That's awesome. But how will we get him there?'

Ngwenya laughed. 'We have a network,' he said. 'Since Mzilikazi's time, the Ndebele people have had many enemies, so we have learned to have friends in many places. Chief Nyoni's grandson is the best wildlife veterinarian in Zimbabwe. He is authorized to sign the necessary papers. He will sedate Khan now and they will leave within the hour for the border. The fuel delivery truck came today and we have already arranged the transport. At the border we also have friends among the customs officials.

'Chief Nyoni's grandson will stay with the leopard until they reach Sawubona. Mrs Thomas said that your game warden, Tendai – did you know that Tendai is an

Ndebele word for thank you? – will take care of him in your wildlife sanctuary until he is well enough to be released into the wild.'

Martine could hardly believe what she was hearing. The magnificent creature now growling in the circle of her arms was going to be living at Sawubona. Even if she rarely glimpsed him, she'd always know he was there. Watching her.

Watching over her.

'But how long will he be able to stay with us?' she'd asked excitedly.

'Perhaps a couple of years, perhaps for ever,' the chief replied. 'We give you our word that we will never send for him or for his sons and daughters until they can once again live without fear in the Matobo Hills.'

The vet had tapped his watch then. 'Time is running short if we are to make the border before nightfall,' he said.

Tears had poured down Martine's face as she realized that, after everything they'd been through together, she and Khan were about to be parted. To the shock and awe of the onlookers, she put her nose to that of the leopard in a sort of Eskimo kiss.

'I'll always love you, Khan,' she whispered, and was rewarded with a final purr.

Minutes later, he'd been sedated and was fast asleep, and Chief Nyoni's grandson and men with a stretcher bore him away. His long journey south had begun.

Chief Nyoni broke the awkward silence that followed. 'I'm glad to have seen with my own eyes that we have appointed the right guardian for the leopard,' he said.

At a word from Martine, Ben left the cavern and she was alone with the chief and Ngwenya.

'I have something for you,' Ngwenya told her. He dug in his pocket and handed her a pink Maglite torch, a Swiss Army knife and one or two other shiny things from her survival kit.

Martine was thrilled. 'Where did you find these?'

'In the hornbill's nest. At the top of the hill, a bees' nest had been knocked down. Magnus's house was behind it. It was full of money and jewellery, like Aladdin's cave.'

'Enough to feed the whole of the Matopos for a year?' Martine teased.

Ngwenya laughed. 'For a year at least.'

'I also found something,' Martine said.

Chief Nyoni sat up straight.

'You found what?' Ngwenya said carefully.

Martine handed him the candle. 'I've left my sweatshirt back there in the shadows,' she said. 'I'll leave it up to you to decide what to do with it.'

She almost ran from the chilly cavern after that, rushing along the tunnel and emerging, blinking, into blazing white sunshine and the waiting arms of her grandmother.

'To think that I was worried about you having a little canter on the white giraffe,' Gwyn Thomas said, hugging her. 'Instead I bring you to the Matopos, where you're chased by hunters, kidnapped by treasure seekers and buried alive with a leopard. The next time I suggest dragging you across the countryside for a so-called holiday, say to me, "Grandmother, I'd much rather stay home and read books and ride Jemmy."'

'Umm, I did try,' Martine reminded her with a grin.

'I know,' said Gwyn Thomas. 'But next time I'll listen.'

They were waiting by the tractor and trailer when Ngwenya and Chief Nyoni appeared at the tunnel entrance. Ngwenya was holding Martine's sweatshirt but nothing else. They were halfway down the hill when there was a muffled explosion. Martine guessed that they'd removed the planks holding up the tunnel roof and triggered a landslide. A dust cloud blasted out of the space where the tunnel had been, and then the whole hillside seemed to buckle and change shape. It was as if the cavern and its contents had never been.

Ngwenya and Chief Nyoni never looked back. When they reached the tractor, Ngwenya handed Martine her sweatshirt.

'Was that the only thing you found?' she couldn't resist asking him.

'The only thing worth keeping,' he said. 'We have love, freedom and enough to eat in the Matobo Hills. That's all we could possibly need.'

The evening star was sparkling over Elephant Rock by the time Martine and Ben made their way down to the retreat. With the coming of night, the intense silence of the Matopos which had so unnerved Martine on their arrival was settling over the hills and valleys, and she thought how much she'd miss it when she was gone. It was quite the most beautiful sound she'd ever known.

The change in Sadie's fortunes and the decision to send the leopard to Sawubona meant that she, Ben and Gwyn Thomas were leaving Zimbabwe earlier than planned. She'd have time to spend reading and riding Jemmy after all. She was ecstatic about that but her heart ached at the thought of leaving the Matobo Hills. She was also wondering whether she'd ever see the leopard again.

'Of course you will,' said Ben. 'Especially if he's going to be living at Sawubona.'

'Yes, but it won't be the same,' Martine told him. 'I won't ever get to fall asleep cuddled up next to him again.'

They were on their way to say goodbye to the six horses when they bumped into Ngwenya, who'd just finished feeding them.

'I wanted to wish you both a safe trip,' he said. 'I am going to the far village with Mercy and Odilo and I won't be back before you leave in the morning. Thank you again for what you did for Khan. And please convey our gratitude to your *sangoma* for providing the medicine that helped Emelia.'

'Come with us,' Martine pleaded. 'Tendai's always saying he could do with an extra pair of hands at Sawubona. Travel back with us. You'd love it.'

Ngwenya laughed. 'I'm sure I would, but no matter

how difficult things get in Zimbabwe, no matter how much we have to struggle, I will never leave the Matopos. My ancestors have walked in these hills.'

'I understand,' Martine said. She shook his hand in the African way, gripping his hand, then his thumb, and then his hand again. 'Goodbye, Ngwenya.'

He smiled. 'No, not goodbye. The Ndebele have a proverb, "Those who once saw each other will see each other again."'

EPILOGUE

The leopard lay with his forelegs stretched out before him, his spotted coat gleaming like liquid gold in the early morning sunlight. In the valley below, the dark shapes of buffalo and striped hides of zebra moved in slow motion across the plain surrounding the lake. Ordinarily the sight of so much food on the go would have made him think of dinner, but today he was only interested in the girl and her rather odd companions, an old woman and a white giraffe. The three of them were watching the sunrise over the lake, and the white giraffe was resting his head on the girl's shoulder.

For reasons that Khan found confusing and nice all at

once, his heart felt soft and full whenever the girl was around. Once, without realizing it, she'd been so close to him in his new den in the Secret Valley that she'd brushed his fur. She'd reacted as if she'd been scalded, she hadn't seen him in the dark. She'd had a bright light with her, but she had chosen not to shine it his way.

He'd followed her into the cave with the pictures after that, and watched from the shadows as she'd met with an exuberant African woman of colourful dress and considerable proportions. After they'd embraced, they'd sat gazing at the pictures and talking. Neither of them looked around, but Khan sensed they knew he was there.

On that occasion as on several others, the leopard could have killed the girl with one bound. She'd trespassed into his territory. But the only urge he ever felt was a burning desire to protect her. She had, after all, saved his life. On the long night in the airless cavern, when he'd suffered ten kinds of agony and felt the strength ebbing from his limbs with every breath, the magic from her hands had been a balm. She'd done something to the wound on his chest (at one stage he was quite sure he smelt honey, which he loathed) and had sort of tricked him into swallowing the most revolting liquid he'd ever tasted.

But afterwards the bleeding had stopped, the pain had gone away, and the hole in his chest had vanished as if by a miracle.

Then something most peculiar had happened. She'd dared to lie beside him and snuggle up to him as if he was her pet cat. She'd even put a hand on his paw. And much to his own bewilderment he hadn't just tolerated her presence because he was too weak to do anything about it, he'd cherished every moment, because the energy that flowed from her was pure love.

It was a strange kind of heaven, sleeping with a small human, but it was heaven nonetheless.

Now they were connected and would be for all their lives. Whether she turned to look at him or not, he knew that she was aware of him. A smile would play around her lips whenever she was close to him and he sensed that she was proud of her part in bringing him to this place of safety.

Since he'd come to Sawubona, the fear that Khan endured all his life had almost gone. There was no reason to be afraid here. It was a wildlife paradise. Still he would always be wary. The girl apart, he'd learned the hard way that humans were not to be trusted. The old woman and the Zulu man who ran the game reserve appeared to be good people and on the side of the animals, but he would always be suspicious of outsiders.

Recently, though, he'd spotted one of his own kind – a female leopard with two cubs. In the coming days he planned to make her acquaintance. He was tired of being alone.

Khan stood up, stretched and prepared to make his way to his hidden sanctuary for his daytime snooze. As he did so, he dislodged a rock. That rock dislodged another rock, which in turn exposed two elephant tusks that had lain undisturbed for more than a thousand years. They tumbled crookedly down the mountain and came to rest with their tips touching, like the head of an arrow.

The leopard saw them land. He paused to sniff them as he moved fluidly down the slope towards his den. They were pointing northeast, beyond the boundary fence of Sawubona, to a place of hot, dry winds, red rippled dunes, and skies like billowing blue canopies.

They were pointing to the land where it all began.

AUTHOR'S NOTE

The inspiration for the last leopard of this book comes from a real leopard, also named Khan who, for the past four years, has resided at Bally Vaughan Bird and Game Sanctuary in Harare, Zimbabwe. Like the fictional Khan, he is, at nearly seventy-five kilograms, one of the largest leopards ever recorded. Khan was orphaned when his mum and dad died of anthrax poisoning, and he is taken care of by Sarah Carter and other dedicated volunteers at Bally Vaughan, who battle against near insurmountable odds to keep Khan and the other precious animals at the sanctuary safe and out of the hands of hunters.

Khan is one of the lucky animals in Zimbabwe. In 2005, when I first came up with the idea for *The Last Leopard*, it was as a reaction against reports I kept hearing about the rise of 'canned' hunting in Zimbabwe, the wicked and widespread practice of putting lions, leopards and other dangerous and hard-to-hunt animals in small enclosures so that 'hunters' are guaranteed a 'kill' or a trophy to hang on their wall. I imagined a worst-case scenario: that the day might dawn when there might only be one last leopard in Zimbabwe. Now, just two years on, the unthinkable is in danger of becoming a reality.

When I set off with my father on a road trip to the Matobo Hills in March 2007 to research this book, I have to admit that I was a little concerned I might have made a mistake deciding to send Martine, Ben and Gwyn Thomas to such a scary place in *The Last Leopard*. On the drive from Harare to Bulawayo, we were stopped at numerous roadblocks by police brandishing machine guns, demanding to know if we were carrying smuggled diamonds – 'I wish!' was my dad's response – or any other contraband. Like Gwyn Thomas, we struggled to find petrol, and the whole of Zimbabwe was stricken by chronic water and electricity shortages.

Entering the Matobo National Park was like entering a totally different country. Martine's first impressions were my first impressions. I had the same sense she does that I'd reached the end of the world. The silence is awesome. The immense, balancing rocks and granite mountains, streaked with jade lichen and chestnut water-stains, are both humbling and breathtaking.

Reviewers of *The White Giraffe* and *Dolphin Song* have described them as magical realism, meaning that they have elements of fantasy and the supernatural in them but also lots of real life and fact. Doubtless the same is true of *The Last Leopard*. But for many people in Africa, and perhaps particularly in the Matobo Hills, cave spirits and the prophesies and healing powers of witchdoctors and *sangomas* are not the stuff of fantasy, but part of every day life – as real as you or I.

For many residents of the Matopos, the cave spirits and guardians of the shrines I've described in *The Last*

Leopard, including the one about the girl who lived under water with crocodiles for seven years, are incontrovertible truths, not fiction. And in Zambia, the sending out of miniature tortoises with coffins or toy ambulances on their backs as a warning or curse is a favourite method of witchdoctors.

What struck me most about the Matobo Hills is that, in spite of the fact that Zimbabwe is in crisis, the gentle, likeable people of this special area seemed almost untouched by the problems in the rest of the country. Life continued much as it did a hundred years before. Peace reigned. Every day, we came across laughing girls, some as young as five, walking six kilometers through the bush to school as if nothing could be more enjoyable or normal.

Yet even for this remote, lovely region, time is running out. The Matobo Hills has always had one of the highest concentrations of leopards in the world, but illegal hunters have moved in and recently one was caught trying to smuggle leopard skins into America. Cheetahs, lions and hippos, animals we thought would be around for ever, are moving onto the endangered list, and the leopard, one of world's most elusive and beautiful creatures, is in danger of being wiped out. Unless we act soon, we'll wake up to discover that there *is* only one last leopard.

Lauren St John
London, 2007

The Elephant's Tale, the sequel to *The Last Leopard*, is now available. Here is a preview of the first chapter.

The first time Martine saw the car, she was high up on the escarpment at Sawubona Wildlife Reserve tucking into a campfire breakfast. She didn't take much notice of it then because Tendai, the Zulu game warden, distracted her by saying something to make her laugh, and because she was too busy savouring the smoky-sweet taste of her bacon and fried banana roll, and also because the car – a black saloon with blacked-out windows – turned around before it reached the distant house and drove away, so she just thought it was someone lost.

It wasn't until the following day, when the black car

came again while she was tending to the sanctuary animals, that she remembered the strange, slow circuit it had made, as if it was in a funeral procession. This time she had no choice but to pay attention to it, because it glided up to the runs housing Sawubona's injured and orphaned animals as if it had a right to be there. The rear door opened and a tall, bald man wearing an expensive navy suit and a watch that could have been hand-crafted from a gold ingot stepped out. He looked around as if he owned the place.

"Can I help you?" she asked, trying not to show how annoyed she was that he and his big car had frightened the sick animals. She was prepared to bet that he wouldn't dream of driving into a human hospital and disturbing the patients, but a lot of people didn't feel that animals deserved the same consideration.

"Oh, I think I've seen all I need to see," he said. But he continued to stand there, a pleased smile playing around his lips. He reached into his pocket for a lighter and a fat cigar, and began puffing away as if he had all the time in the world.

"We're not open for safaris on a Sunday," Martine told him. "You'll have to make an appointment and come back during the week."

"I'm not here for a safari," said the man. "I'm here to see Gwyn Thomas. And who might you be?"

Martine smothered a sigh. She had three very hungry caracals to feed and an antelope wound to dress and she wasn't in the mood for small talk. Added to which, her grandmother had given her all the usual lectures about not speaking to strangers, although she hadn't said any-thing about what to do if a stranger who'd come to Sawubona on official business started plying her with questions. "I'm Martine Allen," she said reluctantly. "If you want to see my grandmother, she's at the house."

"Allen?" he repeated. "How long have you lived here, young Martine? You don't sound South African. Where are you from?"

Martine was getting desperate. She wished Tendai or Ben, her best friend in the world apart from Jemmy, her white giraffe, would show up and rescue her, but Tendai had gone into Storm Crossing to buy supplies for the reserve, and Ben was at the Waterfront in Cape Town seeing off his mum and dad. They were leaving on a Mediterranean cruise. She wanted to tell the bald man that her name and where she came from was none of his business, but she was afraid to be rude to him in case he was an important customer.

"A year," she replied. "I've been at Sawubona for near-ly a year." She could have added, *Ever since my mum and dad died in a fire at our home in Hampshire, England, last New Year's Eve,* but she didn't because she was not in the habit of sharing her private information with nosy strangers. Instead she asked: "Is my grandmother expect-ing you? I can show you to the house."

"A year is a good long time," remarked the man. "Long enough to become attached to a place."

Then he said something that sent chills through Martine. He said: "Shame."

Just like that. Just one word: "Shame."

He said it in a way that made Martine want to rush home and take a shower she was so creeped out, even though he had in fact been perfectly polite and kept his distance throughout. His only crime had been polluting Sawubona's wildlife hospital with his cigar.

Before Martine could come up with a response, he continued briskly: "Right then, I think it's time I had a word with your grandmother. Don't trouble yourself, I know the way."

He climbed back into his shiny black car and was chauffeured away, leaving the sickly smell of cigar smoke and that one weighted word hanging in the air.

"Shame."

Also by Lauren St John

THE WHITE GIRAFFE

Martine is eleven when she goes to live on a game reserve in Africa, a place where mysteries and secrets abound, where the intoxicating magic of the country casts all sorts of spells.

One lonely night, she looks out of her window and sees a young giraffe, silver tinged with cinnamon in the moonlight.

'For a split second their eyes locked, the small sad girl and the slender young giraffe, then the sky went dark. Martine pressed her face to the window, desperate to see the white giraffe again.'

In that instant Martine knows that she is prepared to risk everything for it. The giraffe looks at her as if it is waiting ...

'a spellbinding and mesmerizing debut novel'
Publishing News

DOLPHIN SONG

Through the wild waves came one hundred dolphins . . . leaping, dancing, cavorting . . . their silvery arcs against the midnight ocean and crescent-mooned sky were breathtakingly beautiful . . .

Disaster strikes a school trip leaving Martine and her classmates swimming in shark-infested waters, until dolphins guide them to a coral-ringed island. Here the castaways must learn to survive. Will Martine's secret gift allow her to help both animals and humans when a deadly peril threatens them? And will those powers be with her when she needs them most?

'transports you instantly into the heart of Africa and the landscape so beautifully evoked in her first children's book, *The White Giraffe* . . . beguiling storytelling with a timeless feel.'
The Bookseller

THE ELEPHANT'S TALE

The elephant's whole body trembled; a tear rolled down her face ... Some sixth sense told Martine that the elephant's heart was failing because it had been broken. Her freedom and family had been stolen from her. She had nothing left to live for.

When a sinister stranger threatens Martine's home at Sawubona Game Reserve and her beloved white giraffe, Jemmy, she is determined to try everything in her power to save them. To do that she and her best friend, Ben, must risk their lives by travelling to the Namibian desert. There they uncover a plot so terrible it threatens the existence of every person and animal in the land. Can they trust the mysterious San Bushman boy, Gift? And is the fate of twenty missing elephants linked to Sawubona?

In this fourth, thrilling African adventure, Martine and Ben have just thirteen days to unravel a deadly secret or lose the wildlife sanctuary and animals they love.